THE AUNT
❧ WHO ❧
WOULDN'T DIE

THE AUNT

WHO

WOULDN'T DIE

a Novel

SHIRSHENDU MUKHOPADHYAY

Translated from Bengali by Arunava Sinha

HarperVia

An Imprint of HarperCollinsPublishers

THE AUNT WHO WOULDN'T DIE. Copyright © 2020 by Shirshendu Mukhopadhyay. All rights reserved. Printed in the United States of America. No part of this book may be used or reproduced in any manner whatsoever without written permission except in the case of brief quotations embodied in critical articles and reviews. For information, address HarperCollins Publishers, 195 Broadway, New York, NY 10007.

HarperCollins books may be purchased for educational, business, or sales promotional use. For information, please email the Special Markets Department at SPsales@harpercollins.com.

First published in 1993 in Bengali as *Goynar Baksho* by Ananda Publishers, Kolkata, India.

First published in 2017 in English as *The Aunt Who Wouldn't Die* by BEE Books, Kolkata, India.

FIRST HARPERCOLLINS PAPERBACK EDITION PUBLISHED IN 2021

Designed by SBI Book Arts, LLC

Library of Congress Cataloging-in-Publication Data is available upon request.

ISBN 978-0-06-297634-5

21 22 23 24 25 LSC 10 9 8 7 6 5 4 3 2 1

CONTENTS

THE AUNT ❧ WHO ❧ WOULDN'T DIE

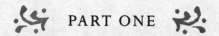 PART ONE

SOMLATA

My husband's name is Chakor Mitra Chowdhury. He's pruned the Chowdhury, though, and is known as Chakor Mitra. At home everyone calls him by his nickname, Fuchu. When we married I was eighteen, and he was blissfully unemployed. By way of skills, he played the tabla and had passed his bachelor's exam. No one in that family had ever held a job. They used to be zamindars, feudal landlords, in East Bengal. The effects of this were evident even at the time of the wedding. People said that despite dwindling wealth, they had enough to ensure their sons wouldn't have to earn a living in their lifetime. The arrangements for the ceremony at the groom's house after the wedding and the jewelry gifted by my in-laws also convinced my family that this must be true.

Aristocratic families on the decline tend to show off disproportionately. They never let go of an opportunity to impress people. I realized from the minor squabbles and arguments in my husband's home after the marriage that they had used up almost all their reserves for the wedding. They had even borrowed money.

My *shaashuri* was a decent woman, especially for a mother-in-law. Mild and sympathetic. She came from a poor, god-fearing family and hadn't been able to blend into this one. One day she made me sit down by her side and said, "It's your fate that Fuchu had to be your husband. He is not a bad sort. But all we have now is for appearance's sake; there's nothing substantial left. I got him married in the hope that his wife's luck will rub off on him. You have to pester him constantly. Do not indulge him in any circumstances. The slightest leniency will mean he will spend all his time in bed. I know the men in this family only too well. Utterly lazy, all of them."

This was worrying. If my husband's fortunes didn't improve after the wedding, would they consider me the source of bad luck?

My *shaashuri* said regretfully, "Do you know how this household runs? With the money that comes from selling land and gold. This cannot go on. If you have any sense, you will groom Fuchu."

"Do you think I'll be able to, Ma?" I said apprehensively. "He's so bad-tempered."

She laughed. "You mustn't fear a man's temper. It's all sound and fury. Pay no attention."

"Will you teach me what I should do?"

"These things cannot be taught. You look smart enough. You will be able to work it out for yourself."

From that very day I developed a sisterhood with my mother-in-law. I had been petrified before the wedding by all the stories one hears about the species, and I felt lucky that she didn't turn out to be a shrew.

But then no family lacks for shrews. My *jaa*—my husband's elder brother's wife—for instance. This sister-in-law was older than me. And a harridan. There was also Pishi, my father-in-law's sister, widowed in childhood. She was the de facto head of the family. She was mollycoddled by both her older and younger brothers because of the tragedy in her life. Her tyranny over the family was remarkable.

The North Bengal town in which my in-laws lived was small, filthy, and congested. There was no variety to life here. Their house was quite a large one. They used to own several houses, even larger, and a lot of land in Pakistan. My father-in-law's father had built them, as was the custom in families of zamindars. Elaborate affairs with many chambers and arches and domes. Nor was there a lack of claimants for a share. When the land on which these houses stood was allotted to Pakistan, all the relatives found sanctuary in this house. At first they were given shelter as distressed members of the family. But later they claimed a share of the house, since it had been built with estate funds. The house was registered to my father-in-law's father; the inheritors were my father- and mother-in-law, my father-in-law's elder brother and his daughter, and my husband and his brother. But that was on paper. Those who had occupied the house had not relinquished possession. The litigation had been going on for a long time, accompanied by quarrels and conflicts. When it came to special occasions, weddings or funerals, though, the entire family was united.

It had taken me some time to grasp the complexities and to get to know each of them individually. They were particularly fond of bragging about their lordly, feudal ways back home. The men in the family were not keen on employment or business. They were more intent on enjoying themselves. But by the time I got married, some of them had had to start earning a living just to survive.

All this is a preamble to my account of my husband. Being the scion of a feudal clan, he had been utterly spoiled as a child, encouraged to be indolent. Since there was no pressure to get an education, he had rolled at a leisurely pace toward a BA degree. He was prone to being short-tempered. No one dared to interrupt him when he practiced the tabla. He was furious if anyone ever woke him up. He would awaken at his convenience. He didn't care to take his wife anywhere, and as for taking her advice or suggestion, that was downright humiliating.

He was quite a bit older than me, thirty-two to my eighteen when we got married. I had not objected to this difference in age, for I had wanted a mature husband. And my parents were so poor that it would be an indulgence to make a fuss about the groom's age or employment status. But, say what you will, my husband now was very handsome, even at thirty-six. Tall, fair, and slim, with a head full of thick hair and attractive in appearance. His looks made it obvious that he was blue-blooded. Given the difference in our ages and his gravitas, I used to address him with the formal *aapni*. The habit has persisted to this day.

A few days after the wedding, when I gauged his mood to be favorable, I said, "Can you tell me why it's not clear whom I'm dependent on in this family?"

"What do you mean?" he asked in astonishment.

"I wish to know who pays for my keep here."

"What sort of question is that? The same person pays for both our keeps."

"But I do not understand who it is."

"Why do you need to? You're getting your meals—isn't that enough?"

I shook my head. "No. That's not good enough. Someone must be paying for it. Who is it?"

He could have been annoyed; he could have scolded me too. At least, that's what I was expecting. But he didn't get angry. With a grave, worried expression, he asked, "You mean you don't know?"

I murmured apprehensively, "Don't be angry, but what I've heard isn't honorable at all. I'm told the family is run on money from selling its gold and land."

He neither confirmed nor denied this. Sitting at a ground-floor window, he was having his evening cup of tea. There was an open drain outside, beyond which stood a wall with the plaster peeling. The room was infested with mosquitoes, and the drain gave off a horrible stench. A depressing, melancholy evening.

Draining his cup slowly, he put it down on the old-fashioned round wooden table and, turning to me, said, "That is correct. I'm assuming you have more to say."

I felt a wave of fear. He looked grim, and his voice appeared even grimmer. But my *shaashuri* had told me not to be afraid. I said, "Family gold is sacred, family land too. I've heard it's not right to sell off either of these."

He was grim but helpless, as his response revealed. Clearing his throat, he said, "I have no idea what to do."

Gathering courage, I said, "Look, the gold won't last forever. The land is probably almost gone too. Shouldn't we be cautious?"

Hiding nothing in his eyes, he said, "Who's 'we'? Do you mean you and me?"

"Of course not," I responded quickly. "We're all in this together, everyone in the family."

Despondently, he said, "The wedding was very expensive too. By the way, why did you bring this up suddenly?"

"You know I belong to a poor family. The poor live a life of hardships. Your family will not be able to bear poverty. You've been brought up in luxury."

"I hope no one here has humiliated you for belonging to a poor family."

"They haven't. But I always feel uncertain because my family is poor."

Gently, he said, "There's no reason to feel uncertain. Your family did not hide anything. We went ahead knowingly. Do you feel I am absolutely worthless?"

"Not at all," I answered hastily. "Perhaps you do not know how much I respect you. Why should you be worthless? It's not that. You could easily earn a living if you wished to."

"But how? All I have is a BA degree. I can get a clerk's job at best. Nothing better, and even that's not easy. I have never considered employment."

"It doesn't have to be a job. You could start your own business too."

"A business! That's for shopkeepers. I cannot possibly do that."

I started laughing at his reaction. "All right," I said, "never mind all that now. This is your time for a walk. Why don't we talk afterward and plan something? That won't upset you, will it?"

He left with a worried expression instead of replying.

Perhaps he was too distracted to pay attention to what I'd said.

Life in a small town was dreary. There was nowhere to visit and no entertainment besides the cinema—and there too only ancient films ran. Gossiping with the neighbors was the only occupation. Even that was forbidden in this family, for it was demeaning to call on ordinary people. As a result, the evenings were depressing and oppressive. I felt like crying. Naturally, I missed my parents. The men could still go out to chat or to play cards, but the women didn't have that option. My *shaashuri* involved herself with meditation and prayers after sunset. My *jaa* couldn't stand me. I was very lonely.

We lived in the southern half of the house. Our share consisted of ten rooms spread over three floors. The other claimants to the property occupied seven or eight rooms in the northern half. There were fewer people on our side. My husband's elder brother, my *bhaashur*, whom he called Dada, had no children. He and his wife, my *jaa*, occupied two rooms on the first floor. My father-in-law's elder brother, the *jetha-moshai* of the family, occupied two as well. My husband and I were in one room on the ground floor, with my father- and mother-in-law in the two others. Pishi lived on the second floor. I wondered what she needed three large rooms for. I went nowhere near her if I could help it. The way she glared at me made my blood run cold. Whenever something went wrong, she screamed so loudly from her second-floor sanctum that everyone in the house could hear her. I've never heard a voice so powerful. She had sent for me once after the marriage and draped a thick gold necklace around my neck. It was going well till then. But then, one day, she was so offensive to me that I wanted to weep at the humiliation of it all. A spirited woman would have taken the necklace off and returned it. I couldn't do it. What she told me indirectly was that she was not at all pleased with her nephew marrying into a pauper's family. I must have been dazzled by the blue-blooded ways of living here. She berated my mother-in-law, who was the root cause for getting a bride from a penniless family, but then again, why not, since she came from one too. And so on.

I often wished I could go up to the roof in the afternoons and evenings. The rooms seemed so dismal, so cavernous, so ghostly, that I simply couldn't bear to spend my time in them. The roof would at least offer me a breath of fresh air. I could take a stroll, sing under my breath. Because it was a common roof, some of the other occupants of the house came up too. There were three or four women of my age—I could have had a chat with them. But I didn't dare go up because of Pishi. Sitting in her room with the door open, facing the staircase, she could make out even if I tiptoed past her.

But I was so miserable in my room that day that despite my fear of Pishi, I made my way to the roof surreptitiously. I was a bundle of worry, apprehension, and anxiety. I did not seem to be experiencing the kind of joy other women felt on getting married. It seemed to me that married life would involve shouldering many burdens, which I might not be equal to.

I was climbing upstairs quietly, on tiptoe. Pishi's room was directly opposite the staircase. The light was switched on. I looked up to find her sitting facing the stairs, as usual. Fair-skinned, with eyes that seemed to devour everything around her. She used to be a beauty. But that beauty had never been worshipped, it had consumed no man, her youth had flowed away in vain. I knew what a litany of regrets her life was. It was no use being angry with fate, with society, with the country. And so her rage was expended on the innocent. Afraid as I was of her, I did not hate her.

I stopped a few steps short. The thought of walking past her actually filled me with fear. Peeping in once more, I was a trifle surprised. Pishi was sitting still, the same way as before. Her eyes were open, unblinking. Her mouth had fallen open. My heart trembled for some reason. This was not a natural sight.

I climbed the last few steps and entered her room.

"Pishima! Aunty! O Pishima!"

No reply. She kept sitting on her massive cane stool, leaning against the wall.

I touched her gingerly, holding my fingers beneath her nostrils. My limbs froze. Pishima was probably dead.

I was about to run downstairs. Suddenly I heard her voice behind me. "Stop. The news can wait."

I jumped out of my skin and looked back. Had she not died after all? But she was sitting the same way. Her eyes bulging, her mouth open. There was no movement of those lips. But I could clearly hear her speak. "Yes, I'm dead, you haven't made a mistake. The wretch is finally gone."

I had never been so terrified in my life. I thought I was going to have a heart attack.

"All of you love the second floor, don't you? You plan to occupy it as soon as I'm dead. And share the jewelry and money amongst yourselves. Not a chance. What are you standing there for? Come here. Come closer."

The order was like a magnet. Drawing me slowly toward her.

"Where do you think you were running off to?"

I couldn't answer. My voice was choked. I could only stare. Pishi's dead eyes were boring into me.

"Take the keys from the end of my sari. Go to the north room. You'll find a locked drawer in the large wooden cupboard. Unlock it. There's a wooden box wrapped in an alpaca jacket. Take it and hide it in your room. No one must know. You think I'm bequeathing it to you? My foot. They'll flock around like vultures once they find out I'm dead. That's why I'm getting rid of it. Keep it hidden. My favorite jewelry—I couldn't wear any of it because of being a widow. I'll snap your neck if you even try it on. Nothing must be touched. Go."

I have no idea how I retrieved the keys from the dead woman's sari or how I got the jewelry box out. I don't remember anything clearly. I was not particularly aware of what I was doing.

Two people saw me as I was leaving with the box hidden in my sari. One of them was Bandana, my *jaa*. She was standing near the staircase, calling for Bhajahari, the family servant. I was practically running by the time I went past her. Observing me without turning her eyes, she asked Bhajahari, "Is that a married woman or a horse? Does she live on trees?"

Bhajahari pressed himself against the wall to let me past. He saw me too.

"What was that she was hiding?" my sister-in-law asked Bhajahari from the top of the stairs.

"Looked like a box," Bhajahari replied.

"A box! Where'd she get a box?"

That was all I heard. Locking myself in my room, I hid the box at the very bottom of my new trunks and turned the lock. I hadn't realized when bringing it downstairs how heavy it was. I did when my arm began to ache later that night.

Should I tell everyone Pishima was dead? But how could I? My heart was trembling so much, I was so out of breath. I felt so confused that I had to lie down for a while. I couldn't even decide if all this had indeed taken place —or if it had, what it was that had taken place.

Pishima never ate a proper meal after sunset, having milk and *khoi* in her room instead. The *khoi* was stored upstairs, while Nanda Ghoshal, the cook, took her a bowl of hot milk.

It was he who came downstairs to tell everyone, "Pishithakrun is looking strange. The signs aren't good."

My mother-in-law went upstairs. Then she shouted to Bhajahari, "Call the men. Send for the doctor. She's done for."

There was no uproar over Pishima's death. No wailing. The menfolk returned home with slightly hurried footsteps. The doctor went upstairs in silence and came back in just fifteen minutes.

I'm sure it looked dreadful that I didn't go upstairs even after hearing of her death. But I didn't have the strength. I was weeping on the bed.

It was my husband who found me in this condition. In great surprise he asked, "What's all this? What are you crying for? Is it for Pishima? How strange."

How strange, indeed. Because no one else in the family was weeping. Not that I was crying in grief for the departed. These were tears of anxiety and terror. Why did fate have to hold such ghastly things for me?

My husband was astonished. Perhaps he melted too, assuming that I was mourning for Pishima. He said, "It's just as well that she's gone. What happiness did she have anyway? She just had those three rooms on the second floor to protect. All she did all day was rummage through her jewelry. No other joy or comfort. But why are you crying so much—when did you get close to her?"

I could not answer. Clinging to him, I said, "Don't go to the crematorium. I can't be here by myself. I'm afraid."

Sitting down by my side, he stroked my head, saying, "I didn't know you were so tenderhearted. You're a very nice girl, after all."

My *shaashuri* called out for me. "Where are you, *Chhoto Bouma,* my youngest daughter-in-law? Come here. You should be here now."

Bhajahari came to summon me. So I had to go up to the second floor eventually. My husband helped me up the stairs. Everyone was astonished to see me cry.

My *shaashuri* couldn't contain herself. "What's all this? What are you sobbing for?"

My *jaa* said nothing, but it was evident that she was scrutinizing me closely. She had seen me go downstairs with a box, after all.

Pishima had been laid out on a mat at the top of the

stairs. All the occupants of the house had gathered. There was a crowd of neighbors. Still, I felt afraid to stand there by the corpse. What if she glared at me?

The entourage left for the crematorium rather late at night. Honoring my request, my husband did not go on the pretext of not feeling well. No one cared.

I couldn't make up my mind whether to tell him what had happened. He wouldn't believe me. I was new here. He might misunderstand me. I was also worried because Pishima had told me to guard the jewelry box carefully. Best not to tell anyone.

Pishima's last rites were completed. People returned from the crematorium. The sun rose.

A family meeting was conducted in the morning in my *shoshur*'s elder brother's room. I was not called. I waited in my room with a beating heart. I was certain they were discussing Pishima's jewelry and the question of who would inherit the second floor.

An hour later, I realized they were going upstairs.

I simply could not recollect where I had left Pishima's keys. All I knew was that I hadn't knotted them back at the end of her sari.

My husband came downstairs an hour later, glowering.

His expression made my heart quake with an unknown fear. After a few minutes of silence, he said, "Pishima's jewelry box couldn't be found."

A barrel of blood spilled in my heart. "Jewelry box?" I asked in a quivering voice.

"Yes. Not a joke. A hundred *bhoris* of gold. Some forty or fifty pure gold guineas alone. Pishima's dowry."

I was surprised. That was more than a kilo of gold. How had I managed to carry such a heavy box downstairs?

Looking extremely worried, my husband said, "Boudi"—our sister-in-law—"is saying strange things. Claims she knows who took it. But won't reveal the name. Baba's saying it must be Nanda Ghoshal. He was the most frequent visitor to Pishima's room."

"Impossible," I interrupted him. "Nanda Ghoshal has been here for years."

"Exactly. And he's never stolen anything."

I made a humble suggestion. "Don't worry about Pishima's jewelry. What does it have to do with us?"

He looked at me in astonishment. "Don't you have any desire for gold?"

I found my voice. "There's not a human being without

desire. From the servant to the saint, everyone has it. Even god himself desires the devotion of people."

My husband stared at me in undisguised wonder. As though he had just begun to discover me. "Excellent," he said. "But where could the box have disappeared to?"

"Let the others worry about that. Pishima's unhappy sighs will always hover over her jewelry. We don't need those ornaments."

My husband appeared to accept this. Then he said, "Ma is saying we should have the second floor cleaned up and move upstairs."

Startled, I said, "Why? We're fine here."

"Hardly. It's dark on the ground floor, infested by mosquitoes. It's so much brighter and airier up there. Much more space too. Dada and Boudi won't move upstairs. My parents won't give up the ground floor because of my father's heart condition. Jetha-moshai is all by himself and doesn't need three rooms. The floor will be unoccupied if we don't move in."

"Let it be unoccupied. I'll be afraid to live there."

My husband smiled. He looked very handsome when he did. I gazed at him, entranced. He said, "Nothing remains of a person after death. What are you afraid of?"

I said, "You know so much more than I do. But I think something of a person does remain even after they're dead. Don't ask me to live on the second floor."

Sadly, he said, "But I've long wanted to move to the second floor after Pishima's death."

"But we're fine here," I said tearfully, "aren't we?"

He didn't insist anymore.

Meanwhile, a furious argument had broken out over the jewelry box. I was worried on not hearing my *jaa* participating. My husband's *jetha-moshai* even mentioned going to the police.

After lunch my *jaa* sent Bhajahari with a message to see her on the terrace. It was autumn, but I remember it being particularly sunny.

Looking at me piercingly, my *jaa* said, "You haven't got rid of the jewelry yet, have you?"

"Why do you say that?" I asked softly.

"You're not naive. It wasn't you who throttled her, was it? I must be careful of you from now on. How horrible."

I was silent. My *jaa* was neither pretty nor plain. Now that she was plump, she no longer had an attractive figure. Her face looked voluptuous, but it also held a hint of cruelty, which became visible now. She said, "I haven't told anyone what you did. There's no need to either. I know Pishima had over a hundred *bhoris* of gold."

"Why are you telling me all this?" I feigned innocence.

"Don't pretend. I'll tell the police if you do. Jetha-moshai is actually informing them. They'll arrest you and take you away on charges of murder and theft."

"I didn't do anything," I said fearfully.

"We'll find out what you've done as soon as your things are searched, unless you've got rid of it already, of course. I've never met a more dangerous woman in my life. You're a terror. I should warn your husband."

Tears sprang to my eyes. To whom could I tell my version? Who would possibly believe it?

My *jaa* said, "Don't expect me to be taken in by tears. Listen, since you *have* stolen them, there's no other way. I want half. Full fifty *bhoris*. I have a trusted jeweler. He will split it equally. No one will know. No one's home at that hour. We'll share it in my room. All right?"

I did not reply.

After some time, she said, "So you want to keep it all to yourself?"

My feet were about to get blisters from the red-hot

sunbaked floor of the roof. She was in slippers. I was barefoot. Ignoring the burning sensation, I said, "You probably suspect me because I come from a poor family."

"There's no question of suspicion. I saw. With my own eyes. You're not only from a poor family, you're from an ill-bred family. There'll be deep trouble if you don't agree to my proposal, I'm warning you."

Flustered, I considered confessing. At least I wouldn't have to bear the burden on my own. Perhaps she wouldn't believe me. So what?

Suddenly I noticed a widow in a plain white sari at the other end of the enormous roof, tugging on a garment hung up to dry. She turned toward me.

I froze even in that heat. It was Pishima.

At that moment one of the young girls who also lived in the house came up to the terrace to dry her hair. She sat down directly opposite Pishima, even looking at her. But there was no change in her expression. I realized she could not see Pishima.

"Why have you turned so pale?" asked my *jaa*. "Are you afraid? That's good. Because if you aren't afraid you will really be in trouble. And if you split the jewelry, there's nothing to fear. I won't tell anyone."

"I don't know anything," I told her. "You can do whatever you like."

I went downstairs. My heart was quaking so heavily at the sight of Pishima that I was about to collapse in my room. My husband usually took a siesta at this hour. He was asleep today too. He would have been extremely surprised to see the state I was in.

I sat quietly by the window. A dove cooed in the silence of the afternoon. A foul stench rose from the drain. My heart thudded.

The afternoon passed this way.

I went to the kitchen to make my husband a cup of tea when he awoke. That was when I heard the sound of someone running down the stairs from the first floor and my *bhaashur* calling for my husband, who ran upstairs.

Bhajahari went out soon afterward to fetch Dr. Rudra.

I stood in silence at the bottom of the stairs.

Bhajahari, who was coming downstairs, told me, "You won't believe it. Boudi has stopped talking."

"Stopped talking! What do you mean?"

"She cannot say a word. All she does is point at someone and moan."

I breathed a sigh of relief. But at whom was my sister-in-law pointing?

No one left the house that evening. Everyone looked grim. They were overwhelmed by the death, followed by this loss of speech.

My husband came downstairs and told me, "Will you go to Boudi, Lata? No one knows why she's suddenly lost her power of speech."

"She doesn't like me," I murmured. "But I'll go if you want me to."

My *jaa* shot up in her bed in agitation as soon as I appeared at her door and then began to moan loudly, pointing at me. I realized she was trying to identify the thief. But no one understood.

My brother-in-law, Chatok Mitra, was a wonderful man, possibly even more handsome than my husband. Fear and anxiety were written all over his sharp features. He asked me helplessly, "What do you think has happened, Bouma? Why is she behaving this way?"

"Perhaps she's trying to say something," I answered softly.

"Say what? Can you make it out?"

I shook my head. "No. But possibly she will tell us once she's recovered."

"Even the doctor can't tell what's happened suddenly. Her tongue has turned to wood. I have never heard of just the tongue being paralyzed."

My *jaa* was staring at me with bulging eyes and jabbing her finger at me repeatedly, trying to draw her husband's attention. I felt afraid.

Her husband, my *bhaashur*, was a harmless, peace-loving man, who inevitably seemed to shrink in the presence of his formidable wife. He seldom left his room, only going out in the evening to meet his friends. Most of the men in the family were worthless and idle-brained, given to sleeping in the afternoon. They grew helpless when in trouble. Lack of use had blunted their faculties. My brother-in-law was so nonplussed by his wife's affliction that he could not interpret her signs.

But there were other ways of communicating even if she couldn't speak. She could always write out everything. Perhaps it hadn't occurred to her because of the sudden paralysis of her tongue. But surely she would realize this soon. And then I would be in trouble.

Suddenly my *bhaashur* took a piece of paper from the desk and handed it to me. "Read this. Can you decipher anything?"

There was only one recognizable letter of the alphabet, *J*. The rest of it was squiggles and lines.

My *bhaashur* said, "She's trying to say something important. She tried to write it out but couldn't. I can't make any sense of it. Only the letter *J* can be identified."

I understood what it meant even if he didn't. "Is her hand paralyzed too?" I asked.

"No. There's nothing wrong with her hand. It's just that she can't write."

I summoned an expression of misery to my face and stood there. It wasn't as though I felt no sympathy for her. However, my fear was much greater. I had no idea what was happening or why. But it was clearly happening.

My brother-in-law said, "Stay with her for a while. I'm going to buy some medicine."

My *jaa* seemed to grow rather fearful and agitated at this and started moaning again. She appeared to be asking her husband not to go. Turning to her, he said, "There's nothing to worry about; Lata is here. I'll be back soon."

He left.

I had never before seen the expression of terror that appeared on my sister-in-law's face. Her eyes seemed to be bursting out of her head, her mouth had fallen open, she was breathing rapidly.

Hurrying up to her, I said, "What's wrong, Didi? Everything will be all right, there's nothing to fear."

She coiled up into a ball in dread. Retreating till her back was against the headboard of the bed, she said in anguish, "Don't kill me. Don't kill me. I won't tell anyone about the jewelry. I swear on the gods. I don't want a share. You know black magic, you've paralyzed my tongue with some trick of yours. I promise you, I will never say a word. I beg of you. Let me go."

Hearing her speak despite a paralyzed tongue confused me again. I stared at her for some time in perplexity. She was sobbing and pleading with me. Her hands shook uncontrollably. She was drowning in her own tears and spittle. I felt miserable. Asking the part-time maid to be with her, I went back to my own room.

The police came in the afternoon to collect testimonies. Bhajahari was about to stammer out something when faced with their interrogation. But for some reason he turned pale and stopped. The police took him and Nanda Ghoshal away as suspects.

My husband and the members of his family began

to discuss and dissect the jewelry theft. I realized that they had expected Pishima's jewelry to pass on to them after her death. It could have replenished the family's depleted store of gold. The men could have lived off the wealth for some years more without having to lift a finger.

I came from a poor family. Even in my dreams I couldn't imagine possessing a hundred *bhoris* of gold. How was I to bear the burden of these riches? I grew more and more restless over the next few days, feeling completely unsettled. I didn't know what to do. It would have helped to share the secret with someone. But my secret was so dangerous that I didn't dare.

I had to cook for the family in Nanda Ghoshal's absence. My *jaa* was unwell and couldn't leave her room. My *shaashuri* wasn't getting any younger. Servants weren't available either. I was relieved to have the opportunity to make the meals. At least I had something to do. It helped me pass the time, keeping me distracted.

One evening I was making mutton for everyone. I was a good cook, praised by everyone. I had just set out the mortar and pestle to grind the spices when I discovered a corner of a white sari behind the door. Someone was standing outside. There were no widows in this family. I froze with fear. My body turned to stone.

I heard a sigh. Undoubtedly, Pishima's voice, though suppressed. "Cooking mutton?"

My heart was trembling. Still, because it was no longer an entirely new experience, I managed to say, "Yes."

"Smells divine."

I sat in silence.

"It's been so long. I've forgotten the taste. Do you cook well?"

"I don't know," I said, my voice faltering.

"It'll be delicious. But you've forgotten the salt. Put plenty."

The white sari moved away. I had an impulse to run away from the kitchen to my room, but I forced myself to stay. For this was probably my destiny. I added salt, though I kept thinking I had done it already.

That night everyone said the mutton was excellent, but there was too much salt. No one could eat it. I was furious.

At night, I asked my husband, "Do you believe in ghosts?"

Seemingly taken aback, he said, "No. Why?"

"Nothing."

31

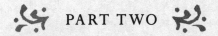

PART TWO

BOSHON

BOSHON

An enormous moon rose over the hill in the evening after our picnic. None of us had seen a moon so large. The peaks, the forest, the river, the gravel paths and sandbars all seemed to submerge themselves in a fairy tale and resurface in a new form. How beautiful the evening had turned out! Many of us began to sing our favorite songs. First just a humming, then out loud, then a chorus.

The cooks and their helpers were busy loading our pots and pans onto the lorry. We weren't going back just yet. We girls held hands and sang and spread out in all directions, singing.

The teachers were shouting, "Don't go too far. We'll be leaving in half an hour."

Who cared for them? An evening like this wasn't going

to come again. Who wanted to abandon such a beautiful spot and such a glorious moon to be cooped up in a hole?

We didn't stick together. A group as large as ours inevitably split into smaller ones. So did we. Four of us strolled along the mountain stream. We had walked here in daylight too, but there was no moonlight then, no reflection of the moon in the water, no enchanted world.

Large boulders were strewn across the river. Just imagine the distance this slender stream had borne all these rocks after breaking them off from the mountains! Now that it was winter, the current was not particularly powerful. How cold and clear the water was!

The four of us sat down, two to a rock. For some time, we sang Rabindrasangeet together, as many songs featuring the moon as we could remember. But the harmonies broke, and we got the lyrics wrong. "Rubbish," we laughed.

Priti was sitting next to me. Supriya and Simantini were on the other boulder. We chatted away happily.

It was freezing. The cold was still bearable, but the north wind shook us to our bones. This icy wind had begun blowing after sunset. It cut through our cardigans and scarves to riddle holes in our bodies. I could feel the cold even in my stomach. Still, how wonderful it felt to be sitting there.

We had split into two groups of two without realizing it. At first we had all been talking to one another, but now it was Priti and me on one side, Supriya and Simantini on the other.

Chatting with Priti was no fun. She would invariably drag Nitish into the conversation. Nitish was her husband-to-be. They had been seeing each other for five years. Now all she could talk about was Nitish. Nitish had given her a bottle of perfume, Nitish would take her to Kashmir after they were married, Nitish had told her after a promotion, "You're very lucky for me," . . . and so on. We knew her Nitish quite well. He was nothing special. But the way she talked made it seem he was one in a million.

What do girls like in boys? Can any girl possibly answer this question? Although our college was coeducational, the girls had come on their own picnic. We no longer went with the boys because they had misbehaved once. Boys drool so much over girls that the whole fun of a picnic is ruined. And it isn't as though it's just at picnics—it's the same every day at the college. The things boys do to be noticed by girls, to appear heroic in their eyes! Some of them even use powder. The well-built ones keep flexing their muscles. We laugh hysterically over all this in the girls' common room.

Priti was itching to start talking about Nitish. Suddenly she said, "You know, Boshon—"

I knew she was going to bring up Nitish now.

I cut her short. "When did you say you were getting married?"

Priti said, "Getting married! Not before April. Might even be June. He won't even get a leave, he's under so much pressure after the promotion. The manager says, 'The office will come to a halt if you aren't here, Nitish.'"

"Will you continue studying once you're married?"

"Of course I will. My father- and mother-in-law have already said, 'Get as many degrees as you can, Bouma. You won't have to do anything for the household. Learn, know, grow.'"

I wanted to laugh. Priti was a mediocre student. She was unlikely to acquire too many degrees. And she was quite inclined to involve herself in household matters. She would be so immersed in home and family after her wedding that she wouldn't even remember her studies.

Priti began her litany about Nitish. I was being transported to an unknown world by the ethereal moonlight. Fragments of what Priti was saying floated into my ears now and then: "You know Nitish, how honest and upright he is. . . . He says, 'You're my guiding force.' They have no demands, not even a watch or ring. . . . Nitish is clueless about money; I'll have to manage everything. . . ."

Why can I not be attached to a man in the same way?

When the entire swarm of girls was on its way to the picnic today, a jeep with a bunch of boys, none of them Bengali, followed us a long way. The teachers told us not to look at them. They whistled, singing songs from Hindi films, gesturing with their hands. How the girls giggled and nudged one another! I was the only one burning with rage.

My *pishi*'s son has a colleague, an engineer, who has just been transferred to our city. A month ago, when I barely knew him, the man suddenly called me to ask, "Are you free?"

I know men inside out. It was obvious from his voice that this was a matter of the heart. "Meaning?" I asked sternly.

He was a confident sort. Chuckling, he said, "Meaning, can I proceed or not? Will you give me a chance?"

I said, "I'm free, and I want to stay that way."

Undaunted, he swallowed the barb and said, "Thank you."

That was the end of that.

Two professors and a doctor had also proposed marriage to me in succession. Not to me directly, but through my father, who had said, "Let me ask my daughter."

I had turned them down.

I still do not know why I cannot trust the male of the species.

Slipping off the boulder, I said, "I'm going for a walk. I don't feel like sitting here."

I wandered off on my own. None of them came along.

I could hear the high voice of one of the teachers, Monica-di. "Come along, girls. The lorry driver won't wait any longer. The contract runs till 10:00 p.m."

I knew everything was guided by rules. I would have to tear myself away from this freedom, this abandon, this fantasy walk amid nature under an exquisite moon, and return home. Just as I will have to dress up in wedding finery one day and take my place on the bride's seat.

Woman and man are supposed to complement each other. I don't agree. I feel I will get by without a man.

I walked into the distance, holding hands with loneliness, my best friend.

Amalesh used to pass our house on his way to school. Tall and thin, with his shirt buttoned all the way up to his throat, dressed in a coarse dhoti, his hair neatly combed. He would march straight ahead, looking neither left nor right. He lived three doors down the road—a structure with bamboo fencing as walls and a tin roof. His father was a teacher at the primary school. He never wore a shirt, only wrapping a flimsy shawl around his bare upper body. Amalesh's mother would come to our house sometimes to borrow some rice or salt when they ran out of it. It was she who told us that Amalesh often went to school without a meal, for there would be no food at home sometimes. She would say regretfully, "The boy's good at studies, but I can't even give him enough to eat. How far can he go on an empty stomach?"

Amalesh was one of the good students at school. But a good student was all he was. Books, and books alone, were his constant companion. He would walk past the football field without the slightest interest in the game. He didn't watch films, didn't chat with friends. All he did was score profusely in his examinations, top his class, and be promoted. "A good boy," said everyone. "A very good boy."

I had been seeing him since childhood. The same clothes. His hair combed the same way. I had never even seen him roll up his sleeves.

I was very young then, seven or eight. Amalesh was a student in grade nine. He was grave for his age. He never visited anyone at home. But his two younger sisters and one younger brother often came to our house for treats during religious festivals. Ma would give them our old clothes, which they would wear happily. Only Amalesh-da was different. He seemed to have nothing to do with other people, as though he had lost his way and arrived in this world, completely indifferent to it.

I remember the neighborhood boys playing football with a tennis ball on the street as Amalesh-da was passing. Caked with mud, the ball suddenly hit him squarely on his chest, leaving a mark on his white shirt. Anyone else would have stopped in annoyance, perhaps scolded them. But Amalesh-da paused for only a moment to lower his head and inspect the mark. Then he went on his way in silence.

I was still in frocks when Amalesh-da got the ninth rank in the entire state in the final school examination. His mother told mine, "All the big colleges in Calcutta want him. I doubt if we'll be so lucky. So expensive."

There was a stir everywhere. Such achievements were not usual in this small town. Two receptions were held to

42

facilitate Amalesh-da, at the school and at Town Hall. I sang the welcome song with two other girls at the Town Hall event. I also had the responsibility of garlanding him and putting a ceremonial tilak on his brow. He had to stoop so that I could reach him. He had his eyes fixed on the floor with embarrassment. No sooner did I put the garland around his neck than he took it off and put it down. There was no glow of pride or accomplishment on his face. He looked as though he'd be relieved if he could hide.

Amalesh-da didn't get around to studying at a Calcutta college. He took admission at a local one and continued walking past our house as before. By way of change, he had become taller, with a hint of a beard. He topped the next exam too, creating a stir all over again.

Sometimes I'd ask his sister Sumita, "Isn't Amalesh-da interested in anything but books?"

"No. That's all he cares for."

"Doesn't he chat with all of you?"

"Hardly. We're terrified of Dada. He makes us so nervous when he's teaching us."

"Does he scold you a lot?"

"No, not at all. But the way he looks at us with those

cold eyes of his is enough. He doesn't talk much. When he does, it's only with Ma."

For some reason, I wanted to find out more about Amalesh-da. What lay behind his aloofness? Was he bad-tempered, or did he lighten up sometimes? A marionette or was he of flesh and blood? But we seldom visited their house. There was nowhere to sit. They used to get so worked up if anyone went over, rushing out to buy something to offer them, always on credit, or to get hold of some sugar for the tea. Their abject poverty made them desperate to welcome guests with great care. Which was why Ma used to say, "Why visit them?"

Amalesh-da's younger siblings, Amita, Sumita, and Alakesh, were all at the top of their respective classes. But none of them were as shy or as obsessed with books as Amalesh-da. Alakesh was a good football and badminton player. Both Sumita and Amita sang and embroidered.

I was approaching puberty. My body and heart were both in turmoil. My first period ushered in both fear and a thrill. A host of unfamiliar windows seemed to have been opened suddenly. My body changed in all sorts of embarrassing ways, and so did the world outside.

That was when I did the stupidest thing in my life. The

embarrassment still makes me want to shrivel. I wrote Amalesh-da a letter. There was nothing objectionable in it. All I wrote was, "I want to meet you. I like you very much."

There was no reply.

I got after my mother. "Tell Amalesh-da to coach me, Ma. He's such a good student."

She didn't object. But having inquired, she said, "He doesn't coach anyone. Very shy, you see."

It could have ended there. I assumed Amalesh-da hadn't got my letter.

But that wasn't the case. One day Sumita told me, "So strange, Dada was asking about you yesterday."

I was startled. "What was he asking?"

"Who you are, where you live, things like that."

Something funny was going on in my heart. Fear, uncertainty, excitement. Amalesh-da hadn't told her of my letter, had he? I couldn't breathe.

"What else did he say?" I asked.

"Did you ever make faces at Dada? Or mock him or something?"

"Why on earth would I do that?"

"He seemed a little angry. So I thought, Oh, no, maybe Boshon was rude to him."

I felt crushed. Angry? Why would he be angry? Was it so bad for a girl to want to be friends with him?

Sumita said, "But then I told him Boshon is wonderful. She's very good at both studies and music. And a quiet girl. Never misbehaves."

Amalesh-da stopped walking past our house. There was a big field across the road. He took the long way around it.

The humiliation seemed to shatter my world. Just when puberty had woven a web of mysteries around me, just when a million lights were playing in the universe that I had conjured up, this heartless affront seemed to be a show of contempt at my blooming womanhood. The world I knew so well was in smithereens. The prolonged despondency of widowhood seemed to rise slowly from the darkness of the netherworld.

Another girl wouldn't have responded this way. It was the age to take wing. Puberty is the time to be fickle, impulsive, shallow. Picking one out of many becomes an impossible task. Many girls like to get attention. But I'm not any other girl, I'm Boshon. I've been born with a strange melancholy in me.

If someone were to ask me today, "Did you fall in love with Amalesh?" I wouldn't be able to put my hand on my heart and say, "Yes." For that would be a lie. I had never exchanged a word with him, not even a glance. Amalesh-da was not handsome or athletic or confident—he was merely a good boy. Girls seldom fall in love with those who are nothing but good boys. I had only wanted to be a friend. I don't know why. When the desire for friendship had arisen, it was only him I had thought of.

The man didn't even answer my letter. He changed his route. He became angry with me. At that age this was all it took to stoke within me a distaste for men.

Amalesh-da left for Calcutta with a scholarship. Then, sometime later, he went abroad. Their ramshackle house was rebuilt properly. Another floor was added. Signs of affluence became visible in the impoverished family. Although they didn't top their exams, Sumita and Amita scored high marks to graduate from school. Alakesh was due to take the exams next. Everyone knew he was bound to get the district scholarship. Their family was quite close to ours now. No one knew what had taken place between Amalesh-da and me. Not that anything to catch people's attention had happened.

And yet, this silent, uneventful incident changed my entire life.

I walked a long way in the moonlight, holding hands with loneliness. I liked solitude these days. This touch of melancholy, this slight sadness, this little weight on my heart of past humiliation, this delicate unhappiness, this trivial needle of envy—all of these garnished my existence. It would have been far too bland otherwise.

The winter stream had spread out a fabric of fine sand. The moonlight was almost glaring. It was bright enough for even a pin to be spotted. I stopped at a bend in the river. A solitary hill stood on the other bank. Silent, mute, still. The water gurgled past my feet. Even the gravel on the riverbed was visible in the moonlight. As I gazed at the unending emptiness all around, it suddenly occurred to me how good it was that I was so alone, that there was no one in the world waiting for me. This was best for me.

Teacher Shobhana's voice blew in on the wind, sounding like a wail of despair. "Boshon, Boshon, where are you? Everyone's in the lorry. Come at once."

I went back, depositing a secret sigh with the moonlight and the loneliness.

The teachers scolded me roundly. "Such an irresponsible girl. Have you any idea how late it is? Just one person holding everyone up. I don't know what's wrong with you girls these days."

I enjoy being by myself, but I don't mind being in a group of people either. I lose myself in the laughter, jokes, and conversations. I seem to be two people. Hoisting my sari and clambering onto the lorry was a matter of much merriment. The seven teachers sat on a sheet while we girls squeezed in amid the pots and pans. Nine or ten of us sat on the roof of the cab. Some had to stand. It was quite crowded. When the teachers told us not to sit on the cab, some of the girls climbed down again and perched on upturned pots and buckets, which wouldn't stay steady because of their handles, rattling as the lorry moved. And everyone rolled with laughter.

After a while, the laughter gave way once more to songs. The lorry was approaching the town. We had left the ethereal valley of the moonlight to advance toward our constricted homes, our cubbyholes. Why did humans have to learn how to build houses? In ancient times they used to live in mountains and caves, beneath the trees. Perhaps I had also been a cavewoman many births ago, hunting animals with stones, roasting their meat, wandering around at will amid hills and forests. An unshackled life.

Our songs and chatter and laughter took us halfway on our return journey. It would be past ten by the time we got into town, after which we would go to our respective homes. But there was uncertainty in every destination. Just as Teacher Bandana glanced at her watch and told Teacher Shikha, "We should be back in an hour," the lorry began to emit hiccups.

This too made us giggle.

Shobhana said in annoyance, "I'm sick of all this giggling. What's wrong with the lorry? Ask the driver."

There was no need to ask. The lorry stopped at the side of the road. The driver and his assistant disembarked, opened the bonnet, and peered inside by the light of a torch.

"What's the matter, Driver?" asked Madhuri-di.

"No acceleration. Dirt in the diesel," answered the driver.

"We'll go on, won't we?"

"Of course. Let me fix it."

"It won't take too long?"

"Five minutes."

Five minutes stretched into fifteen. Then half an hour. The anxious teachers looked over the railings. "Why aren't you telling us what the matter is? We're responsible for all these girls here. Will the lorry move at all?"

The driver said uncertainly, "We're trying, Didi. The suction is acting up."

Shobhana was infuriated. "Why are you people so callous? How could you do the trip with a defective lorry? What will we do now? There's still a long way to go."

"These are machines. You can't always predict how they'll behave. It was overhauled just last week."

Soon we realized that the lorry was in serious trouble. The girls stopped giggling. The teachers vented their anger.

Indira-di said, "Even if the lorry is stalled we do have to go back. Stop some other lorry, Driver."

The helper tried to do just that. Because it was late at night on a holiday, however, there were very few trucks on the road. One of them did stop. It was packed with tea chests. The driver got out, tried to help in fixing our lorry, then gave up after some time and drove away. Two others didn't even stop. A private car did, but it held four drunken men. One of them said, "Where are all these women being trafficked, my friend? Are you dispatching them to Abu Dhabi under cover of the night?"

One of the relatively less drunk passengers said, "Can't you see they're from decent families? A picnic party."

The third one said, "Pour a pint into the fuel tank, Driver Saab, the lorry will fly."

They didn't stay any longer. Their driver drove off.

About an hour later the driver tried to get the lorry to start. The vrooming sounds gave us some hope, but the lorry didn't budge.

Indira-di wailed, "But it's very late already. What shall we do?"

The driver said in great embarrassment, "Battery down."

Shobhana said, "What to do, then?"

"Just needs a push."

"Who's going to push?"

"Will the teachers help? Nothing much, just a little shove."

As soon as we heard that, all of us offered to help. Why couldn't we push the lorry? Were we helpless? Hadn't we eaten mutton for lunch? We leaped to the ground. The teachers made noises of protest. "Careful! What if the lorry starts moving suddenly? This isn't a job for girls."

The lorry was like a house. Even with all of us pushing, it didn't budge an inch.

Shikha-di said from the back of the lorry, "Wait, let us get off too. And listen, all of us have to push together. Stop giggling. You can't summon the strength to push if you keep giggling."

This made us giggle even more.

The teachers climbed out of the lorry. Indira-di said, "Haven't you seen how laborers do it? They go 'Hey-ho, hey-ho' when they're fixing sleepers on railway lines. We have to do something like that."

She launched into a line from the song "Kharabayu Boy Bege": "I'll hold the tiller, you raise the sail, all together now, hey-ho, pull hard, hey-ho. . . ."

We split our sides laughing.

Shukla said, "We aren't pulling, teacher, we're pushing."

"Same thing."

It was true. We were laughing so hard that we had no strength to push. The lorry couldn't even feel us pushing.

Eventually, we did stop laughing. The lorry began to roll forward slowly, jerking every time the driver tried to start the engine.

Vroom, vroom, *vroooom*! Startling all of us, it suddenly burst into life. We cheered loudly.

The journey resumed along the road through the jungle.

Sitting precariously in one corner, I found myself sinking into sadness. We were going back. Why were we going back?

I had no idea when Priti had sat down next to me. Tearfully, she said, "Boshon, where do you think the ring from my left ear fell off?"

"How would I know?"

"The hook was loose. Must have fallen off when we were pushing the lorry. What will I do now?"

"Why are you so worried?" I said. "Such a lovely picnic, such a glorious moon—you can sacrifice your earring to the occasion."

"You're weird. Ma will scold me so much."

"Let her. Your Nitish will give you lots of jewelry."

Priti said indignantly, "Yes, I know how much jewelry he'll give me. What do I tell Ma now?"

One lost earring had made the night, the moon, this immense richness of the evening meaningless to Priti. She sat there glumly. These things were not meant for girls like her. For Priti there were dingy rooms, husbands and families, a busy household.

And for me? I didn't know.

I felt a stab of pity for her. She was looking so despondent. "Can't you assume the earring isn't lost?" I asked her.

"How can I assume that? How is that possible?"

"Why not? The earring must still be lying where it fell. Right?"

"That's true."

"Then it certainly is somewhere. Just imagine you chose to leave it there."

"What rubbish. Makes no sense, the things you say."

Returning home late that night, I went to bed after a mild scolding. I couldn't sleep till much later. I felt drunk. My little box was brimming with happiness today. I couldn't shut the lid. How was I to sleep? It was like when Ma couldn't make all the sugar in the packet fit into the tin. She tried to pack it all in, but still it overflowed. So annoying. I was in the same situation.

Priti had lost an earring. And I? I had left my entire existence behind in that lonely moonlit valley! I could feel myself wandering around there still. Flowing hair, slow footsteps, a song in my throat, the giant moon sprinkling gold dust everywhere. The muted sound of waves breaking on the pebbles in the river. As beautiful as a deep, impenetrable dream.

I'm certain I'll be a ghost when I die. I'll haunt the world's remotest mountains and forests and sand beaches.

I'll burst into laughter when the storm breaks. I'll drench myself in the rain. I will never be born as a woman again.

Suddenly in the dead of night I could hear the mad woman who had married into the Chatterjee family singing tunelessly, "Save your money, save as much money as you can, eat no honey, work isn't funny, save your money, save your money. . . ."

I couldn't stay in bed. My heart bled for her. Her room was directly opposite my window, separated by only a couple of yards. When Sreemoyee was married into the family four years ago, everyone predicted she would have to work to the bone. The Chatterjees were misers, and it was practically a family trait. The grandfather was a miser, the father was a miser, the son was a miser. Charu Chatterjee was a lawyer. It wasn't enough for his clients to pay their fees; he also kept himself abreast of what vegetables they grew in their gardens, even raiding their homes. Charu Chatterjee earned handsomely. His son Sumit was a government officer. Rice starch, vegetable peel, wheat husk—they didn't throw away any of it. The new bride couldn't bear such intolerable miserliness. She went mad when having her child. The baby in her womb was a large one, making a normal delivery difficult. Frightened, the midwife had asked for a doctor and a cesarean delivery. Eventually they did take her to the hospital, but there was no room. There were many private nursing homes in this town, but the Chatterjees didn't try to go there. Sreemoyee was close to dying in the hospital corridor. Finally, a young gynecologist who saw her condition during the morning rounds arranged for a cesarean delivery in the hospital. The baby did not survive. Sreemoyee did. But the combined shock of her husband's and father-in-law's miserly behavior and the loss of her child sent her over the edge. Now all she did was laugh and cry and sing. But she did the household chores too.

Opening the window, I gazed at their house. The window opposite mine was open too. Sreemoyee was standing there despite the cold, her hair undone. She was the only daughter of a widow. Her mother's brothers had spared no expense during her wedding. Sreemoyee's mother had died two years ago. Now she didn't even have a home of her own. She was burning, she was dying.

Sometimes I shouted out through the window, "Can't you set the house on fire, Sreemoyee? Sprinkle some kerosene and light a match. Let them all burn to death."

Ma had scolded me when she heard. The Chatterjees

were furious with me. Fat lot I care. I'll set their house on fire one day even if Sreemoyee doesn't.

Softly I said, "Sreemoyee!"

She stopped singing. After a silence, she said, "What?"

"Why aren't you asleep? Who sings at this hour?"

Sreemoyee said, "What a moon tonight."

"Do you like the moon?"

"No. I don't like anything. I want to cry."

"Go to bed. Sleep."

"I'm going to turn into a fairy and fly away tonight."

"Fly away where?"

"Up in the air. Have you been on a plane?"

"Never."

"What's it like?"

"I don't know."

"Is it scary?"

"I'd be scared stiff. Go to bed."

"Not going to bed now. What a moon."

Sreemoyee began singing again, "Save your money . . ."

I lowered my voice. "Sreemoyee!"

"What?"

"Don't you know any other song?"

"I do."

"What song?"

"Can't remember."

"This is an awful song. Sing a nice one. You know the one about the moon's smiles?"

"No!"

"I'll teach you."

"I shan't learn it."

"Don't sing this one anymore. It's awful."

"It's the only one I can sing."

"Do they tell you to save money all the time?"

"Money is so valuable."

I closed the window with a sigh. Splashing some water on my face in the bathroom, I decided I would never get married. No way. It was better to die. And if I could turn into a ghost, I would go off to the valleys, the mountains, the forests, the rivers, singing with my hair flowing. . . .

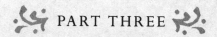

PART THREE

SOMLATA

s that *shuntki* you're cooking? Smells delicious."

"Of course not. We don't eat *shuntki*." She of all people knew that only poor families eat fish that way.

"*Eyh!* Queen Victoria! We don't eat *shuntki*. Why not? Hot and spicy with chilies and onion and garlic. Why don't you eat it?"

"It stinks."

"*Eeeeh!* It stinks! Where's the smell coming from then?"

"Next door, perhaps."

"If they can, why can't you? What are you putting on airs for?"

"Do you like the smell?"

"I'm a widow, remember? How can I say I like it? It's a sin. What are you cooking?"

"Fish."

"What kind?"

"Koi with cauliflower."

"What sort of seasoning?"

"We don't use seasoning for fish."

"Fat lot of cooking you know. You have to use five-spice *paanchphoron*."

"All right."

"Also, some oil, a pinch of sugar, a little baking soda. Just see how it tastes."

"All right."

"Eat all the fish you can. Two months more."

My heart quaked. Pishima was standing outside the open kitchen door. It was dark there. Only her white sari was visible. Looking in her direction, I asked, "Why did you say that?"

"You'll become a widow, you see."

My eyes began to well with tears; waves crashed against my heart. I said, "Why will such a thing happen, Pishima?"

"Why not? Why should I be the only one to suffer? Why not you too?"

"What have I done, Pishima? Have I committed a sin?"

"What sin did I commit? Are you pregnant?"

"I don't know."

"It'll die too if you are. No need for a child. Don't sleep with your husband. Stay apart."

I trembled with fear. The white sari vanished. I was so unmindful that the fish curry was burned to cinders. No one could eat it.

At night, I asked my husband, "Do you believe in ghosts?"

He said in surprise, "You asked the same thing the other day. Why?"

"Tell me."

"No, I don't. There's no such thing as ghosts. Are you afraid of ghosts?"

"I don't know. Maybe I am."

"You're a strong woman. Then why this strange fear?"

"It's not exactly fear. I can't quite explain."

Embracing me intimately, he said, "There's nothing to fear."

We made passionate love that night. Then my husband went to sleep. I tossed and turned in anxiety.

There was no knowing when she would turn up. But it was usually when I was cooking in the evening to give me incorrect advice. The fish and meat often ended up with clumps of hair, ash, or dead lizards in them. Giving the mattress an airing to get rid of an infestation of ants, I discovered sugar sprinkled all over it.

One day I said, "What's all this you're doing, Pishima?"

"And why shouldn't I? What happiness did I ever get here?"

"I've heard you were the head of the family."

"My foot. They were good to me only because of the jewelry box. They let me stay here because of the gold. Or I'd have been kicked out long ago."

"What do you want now, Pishima?"

"I want your husband to die, your child not to be born, you to be a widow. And then I want you to die too. I want everyone to die. Let the world be destroyed. Let every home be set on fire."

"*Maago!*" I said. *Mother!*

"Oh, you didn't like hearing that, did you? Die, Maagi, what's wrong with that? When you're like me, you'll know there's no happiness unless the entire world turns to ashes."

My husband didn't die two months later.

One day Pishima asked from the shadows where she lurked, "How does it feel, eh?"

"How does what feel?" I asked.

Pishima said with a touch of embarrassment, "Don't pretend you don't understand. All those things you do with your husband, what else?"

"Shame on you, Pishima."

"*Ish*, what a shrinking violet. Is it a crime to ask? Married at seven, widowed at twelve. I wasn't even old enough to understand. By the time my body woke up my hair had been cropped and I was reduced to one meal of rice a day and fasting on Ekadoshi. How will you understand what I went through? Tell me what it's like."

"It's good."

"Damn you, you bitch. Everyone knows it's good. Give me details."

"It's embarrassing, Pishima."

"Then die. Die, die, die, die. Die right now."

"*Omaago*! How can you talk like that?"

"Of course I will."

⁂

We were sliding toward poverty. The money was running out. Expenses were mounting. One day my husband said, "You were right. We should do something. But what?"

"Why not start a business?"

"Become a shopkeeper after the lives we've led?"

"What's wrong with that? Everything is acceptable in an emergency."

"Where will I get the money?"

"I got plenty of jewelry as wedding gifts. All of it from your family. Pishima gave me a necklace that must be at least ten *bhoris*. I have a pair of bangles, not less than five *bhoris*. A diamond ring."

"What are you saying? You want me to sell all this?"

"No, why should you sell it? I will and give you the money."

"What will that leave for you?"

"It will leave you for me."

Pishima appeared that evening.

"So you sold the necklace I gave you."

"Yes, Pishima."

"How dare you? You'll die of leprosy."

"I sold it because I don't want to die."

"Remember what I did to Bouma?"

"I do."

"Should I take care of you too?"

"No, Pishima. Forgive me. We have no choice. No one sells gold if there's another way."

"You're a lowlife, you're capable of anything. I'm sparing you because you're supposed to be married."

"Supposed to be married? What do you mean?"

"If only I hadn't been a child widow, I'd have shown everyone how to take care of your husband. But the wretch was already halfway to senility when he got married. Bad lungs on top of that. Died just like that."

"What would you have done if he had lived?"

Pishima said shyly, "So many things. I'd have given him so much love, just like you do. I'd have looked after him all the time."

I smiled.

She said, "Gold was at twenty rupees a *bhori* when I got married. How much is it now?"

"A thousand."

"What! You're a witch. How will you digest so much money? Do you know there's a curse on gold? That shop of yours will perish. How could you turn a man from this family into a shopkeeper? You'll be buried in a bucket of filth in hell. You'll have a stillborn baby, take my word."

My heart trembled. My husband established a shop with a capital of just a few thousand rupees. A great deal of money went simply into setting it up. After it was done up, there wasn't enough money left to buy the merchandise. He borrowed some and got going somehow. But he lacked experience, he botched up the accounts, it hurt his pride as a scion of an aristocratic family to speak deferentially to all kinds of customers. On top of which, friends and people he knew bought from him on credit. An assistant was hired, but he ran away a month later, after stealing some money and a dozen silk saris.

In utter despair he said to me, "This can't go on. I'm a failure."

But I didn't lose hope. If we were deep in trouble, if we ran up huge losses, I always had Pishima's hundred *bhoris* of gold jewelry. I would sell it if need be. Survive or perish.

"There are always ups and downs in business," I told him. "You mustn't worry. I'm by your side."

"You had to sell your cherished ornaments."

"You are my greatest ornament."

My husband was a serious sort of person. After a short silence, he said, "No one has told me anything like this in all these years. I am astonished by your love for me. Why do you love such a useless person? I realize today how worthless I am, completely lacking in abilities."

I said softly, "You have practically given up playing the tabla. Your instruments were gathering dust. I've dusted and cleaned them. Play it again—you'll feel better. I'll play the tamboura with you."

He was extremely pleased by the proposal. He grew cheerful after spending a long time with his tabla. "You've come up with an effective remedy," he said.

My world revolved around him. That I loved him was neither for his good looks nor for his qualities. I loved him because I couldn't possibly not. It was this love that kept the lamp alive in my heart. I could never tell anyone all this. Not even my husband. I lived and breathed for him. But I also got alarmed if he became too wrapped up in me. His masculinity would be deflected if he became henpecked. No one respected or valued a henpecked man, and they didn't have a personality either. Sometimes he would be reluctant to go to work, saying, "Never mind the shop today, I want to spend the day with you." I would jump up at once, saying, "Then I'll have to go."

I used a combination of coercion, cajoling, strictness, and love to keep him busy. These people were lazy and self-indulgent by nature. Loosening the reins even a little made them lethargic.

71

No one in the family had approved of the shop. Especially not my father-in-law, my *shoshur*, and my husband's brother, my *bhaashur*. There were constant clashes. Sending for his son, my *shoshur* said, "How can a gentleman become a shopkeeper? You've brought disgrace on the family. How shameful it is to meet other people now!"

My *bhaashur* was extremely annoyed too. He would often declare at the dinner table, "It's difficult to walk down the road. My friends sneer at me."

My father-in-law's brother was not very vociferous, but from time to time he would say, "This is prostitution. Being a whore."

They knew my role in setting up the shop. One day my *shaashuri* sent for me. "All of them are furious with you. But frankly, I don't blame you at all. I am happy that Fuchu isn't vegetating, that he's not rusting anymore in mind and body. Your *shoshur* may have a talk with you this evening. Don't be afraid."

But I did feel afraid. I seldom spoke to him or to my *bhaashur*. Was I capable of explaining?

I was distracted all afternoon. Suddenly, sensing someone's presence in the room, I discovered the familiar white sari in a corner. The same shadowy figure.

"Now the fun will start. Your *shoshur* is very bad-tempered. He will whip you today."

I said, "Let him."

"Listen. If you do as I tell you you'll escape unscathed."

"What should I do?"

"Your *shoshur* has a secret. Do you know what it is?"

"No."

"He has a kept woman. Her name is Chameli. Lives near the canal. He has lavished a lot on her. Money, jewelry. If he threatens you, tell him, 'I know about Chameli.' He'll turn defensive."

I knew aristocratic families had vices like these. There was nothing to be surprised at if my father-in-law had a mistress. I was silent.

Pishima said, "So you won't do it?"

"I can't say such things."

"Of course you can't. Want to know more? Your husband has one too. Her name is Kamala. You think he's deeply in love with you? Nonsense. What beauty or accomplishments do you have anyway? You think you've got him in your pocket. Rubbish. He visits Kamala whenever he gets the chance."

I was electrified. My eyes filled with tears.

Suddenly I heard Pishima crying too. "Each of them is worse than the other. All bastards, swines. You think your *shoshur*'s brother or your *bhaashur* are innocent? Both have concubines, even two. A wife at home means nothing to them. You think they're satisfied with their wives? They were debauches, and they left me to play with my jewelry box at home. Because I was a fool, I fell for their game. There was a servant named Ramkhelaon. I was in full bloom. A high tide in my body. Ramkhelaon was a young man. So manly. Are you listening?"

"Don't tell me any more, Pishima, I beg of you."

"*Ish*, what a paragon of virtue. Why should I not tell you the story? Listen carefully. Eventually I gave Ramkhelaon a hint. He came in the dead of night. I was full of the desire to sin, to forget about a widow's abstinence. My body was on fire. I was lurking like a tigress. And that idiot slipped on the staircase and fell down. What a scene! Your *shoshur* and his brother thrashed him within an inch of his life and threw him out. Their pious child-widow sister remained starving. And the very next day they put perfume on their wrists and went off to their mistresses. Are you listening?"

"I am, Pishima."

"Are you crying? Cry away, cry to your heart's content.

Let your heart burn. If you want to survive, tell your *sho-shur* to his face, 'I know about Chameli.' Understood?"

"I can't do it, Pishima."

"Then die, die, die at once. Become a leper. Let your father die, let your mother die, let your brothers and sisters die, let your children die."

I couldn't stop weeping. My chest felt like a ton of bricks.

"You're burning, aren't you? Now light a fire under their arse. Let them burn too. Let the family go up in flames. Your brothers-in-law, your husband—shove poles up their backsides. Let them die of cholera, of leprosy. Are you listening?"

I couldn't answer.

"When you burn like I do, you'll learn."

Everyone went into the drawing room downstairs in the evening. My *shaashuri* came to fetch me. "Come, Bouma. They've sent for you. Stay calm."

My heart was weighed down.

Clearing his throat, my father-in-law said, "Sit down, Chhoto Bouma. There's something serious to discuss."

I did not sit. I remained standing by the door, the end of my sari a cowl over my head.

He said, "All this business of shops is humiliating for our family. This isn't respectable at all. How can someone from this family be an ordinary shopkeeper?"

I stood in silence with my head bowed.

My *shoshur*'s elder brother said, "We've also heard that the shop was financed by selling the jewelry you got as dowry. That jewelry represented the benedictions of your elders. Do you not value blessings? They have been insulted by your selling the jewelry."

My *bhaashur* said, "And why is it necessary to set up a shop? There are other lines of business too. How much can you earn from a shop? I heard there have been heavy losses in the very first month. An employee stole money and ran away."

My *shoshur* said, "We want to hear your viewpoint too. Times have changed. Wives' and daughters' opinions had no value earlier. They have become eloquent today. You may speak."

I said nothing at all. They were furious right now. Nothing I said would be acceptable to them.

He continued, "It is true that the theft of Pishima's jewelry has put us in some trouble, but that will pass."

I did not understand how he expected the financial

crisis to pass. Finally, I said, very softly, "Rice and oil became more expensive last month. Our budgets are tighter. We've run up two months' debt with the grocer."

"I am aware. Some more land and a pond in Pakistan will soon be sold. Once that money is here, we have nothing more to worry about."

I went to my room. My husband joined me a little later. He told me, "They suggest the shop be sold."

Softly, I told him, "You needn't go to the shop tomorrow. I will."

"You!" He stared at me openmouthed.

Looking at him with moist eyes, I said, "I have something else to tell you today. Promise me you won't be angry."

In surprise he said, "Yes, tell me."

"Do you love another woman?"

"What are you saying?"

"Is her name Kamala?"

He seemed to shrink. How helpless the handsome, well-built man looked! I said, "Don't hold yourself back. If you need Kamala, marry her and bring her home. I can tolerate it."

He slumped on the bed, hiding his face in his hands. He was ashamed.

My eyes flowing with tears, I said, "There's no need to visit her in secret. Where secrecy involves fear and shame and revulsion, that's where vulnerability and sin reside. I cannot let you commit such a sin."

He sat with his face buried in his hands for a long time. Then, lifting his distressed, embarrassed eyes, he said, "Who told you about Kamala?"

"Is that important?"

Emitting a sigh, he said, "There's no question of marrying her. I've hardly ever visited her since you came."

"Forgive me for what I'm saying. I want you to be happy. Most important, I want to be proud of you. You are my glory. Don't conceal anything. You must understand that I am incapable of thinking ill of you."

"You don't hate me?"

"Not in the least. Please do not apologize to me. Do not stoop."

Looking at me in wonder, he said, "I don't believe it."

"What don't you believe?"

"That you are a flesh-and-blood human being."

"You saying that is tantamount to my sinning. More important, you will become small if you consider yourself guilty constantly."

Emitting yet another sigh, he said, "Then let me tell you, Biren may have stolen money from the shop, but he did not take the saris."

"Then who did? Was it Kamala?"

"Yes, she came to the shop one day and took them. Can they be retrieved now?"

I shook my head. "No. Twenty silk saris are not worth a fortune. Kamala can keep them. She will get a lot more if you marry her."

He bit his tongue. "Why are you bringing up marriage?"

"Then what should I conclude?"

"What has happened will not be repeated."

Gently, I said, "Men are inconstant and fickle. I will not take it to heart if you do the same thing again. Only promise that you will not conceal it from me."

He only shook his head in mute astonishment. Fear or perhaps dread appeared in his eyes. He could no longer think of me as an ordinary woman.

But I knew that an ordinary woman was just what I was. All I wanted from the world was what was due me. There would always be opposition, invisible enemies, crises, destiny—all of which would have to be negotiated. They mustn't make you stop thinking sensibly. What claim could

I have laid to my husband if I had quarreled with him over Kamala or made a scene? His hurt male ego, his injured pride, would have hardened him. He would have insisted on visiting Kamala. I would have died of jealousy. I preferred to keep the door open for him. He could visit any woman he wanted. But he wouldn't feel the need anymore.

I kept waking up that night, and I could hear Pishima wandering around my room, muttering, "Die, die, die, become a widow, may you have leprosy. . . ."

I did not protest publicly against my *shoshur* and *bhaashur*. But I succeeded in instigating my husband. I told him, "If you don't want to go to the shop, I will. We have to be alive to preserve our honor."

He said, "Very well. I shall go."

I shook my head. "You may feel uncomfortable on your own. I will go with you."

"What will the family say?"

"They will be affronted at first, but then they'll stop. They'll get used to it. They can also see that the times are changing. Even if they protest, once they see we're making money from the shop, they will support us."

"You think so? I think you're never wrong. Very well, that's what we'll do."

I don't give in to emotions. I have fears, I feel anxiety, I make the effort to move the pieces of real life around in a way that helps me survive. When we began working in the shop together, genuine love grew between us amid all the blows and counterblows, ups and downs, profits and losses. We developed trust, dependence, mutual respect.

He found it impossible to maintain the books, let alone keep track of the inventory, sold on credit constantly. As long as someone else was running the shop, he had depended on that person completely. And so the shop had fallen on bad days rather quickly. I didn't know how to maintain the books either, let alone keep track of inventory. But does anything get in the way of a woman who becomes a mother for the first time without knowing anything about how to bring up a child? The shop was like my baby. It took me some time to explain this to my husband. It took me even longer to get him to brush off the stardust of aristocracy and become as industrious as a laborer. The shop began to turn a profit.

Buying goods from wholesalers in this town did not offer the chance for large profits. But buying from Burrabazar or Manglahat in Calcutta did. I persuaded my husband to do this. Being lazy and a reluctant traveler, he didn't agree at first. I accompanied him on the first two occasions. Then he began doing it on his own.

People's tastes changed every day. The demand for particular colors or designs peaked at different times. One had to make an intelligent bet. Our purchases kept this in mind. Profits grew.

My *shoshur* made an unexpected raid on the shop one evening. Pleated dhoti, crimped panjabi, a shawl draped around his neck, a cane in his hand, new slippers on his feet. He looked around briefly with contempt. The shop was crowded. He watched the sales for a while and then left.

He came back a few days later. I offered him a chair. He accepted it.

"Brisk sales."

"By your grace."

"Not mine, Bouma, I never offered you my blessings. I cursed the shop, if anything. Neither works. A sinner, you see."

I was silent.

He said, "I don't approve of your disobeying us. But the ultimate result appears to be beneficial. How much do you make every month?"

"Three or four thousand."

"That's a lot of money."

Since his male ego and his self-respect would be injured, I did not tell him that the money from the sale of land and the pond in Pakistan had not yet turned up, that there was no gold left to sell, and yet the household was running— which was not by magic. There was no need to tell him either. He knew. And because he did, he began to visit the shop every day.

The contemptuous smile had disappeared from his face. Two silk saris were sold for two thousand rupees each in front of his eyes.

He stirred in his chair. "How much profit from those two saris, Bouma?"

Smiling shyly, I said, "We have to consider the cost price, allocate the transport cost, rent, electricity bill, and employee salaries and then work out an average to price the sari."

"*Uff*, it sounds very complicated. How do you calculate all this? We only blew our money, never stopped to count it. All this is the work of lower-class people."

I said softly, "Our profits from those two saris is six hundred and thirty rupees."

Startled, he muttered, "Six thirty. From just two saris."

He went home, nurturing his astonishment with a worried expression.

He sent for me a few days later and said, "I know you have to rush to the shop every morning. I am free at that time. I will go there with Fuchu."

I was uneasy about this. His was a feudal disposition. What if he was rude to customers? I said, "You don't have to take the trouble. It doesn't suit you to work in a shop."

He smiled. "Don't worry. Let me try to make sense of the whole thing. I thought it over. I have made no use of this thing called the brain that god gave us. Let me try to shake off some mental lethargy in my old age at least."

I did not stop him. He began. Returning home in the afternoon, my husband said, "You won't believe what happened. Baba quoted inflated prices for all the saris. Two customers ran away. Why did you send him? He didn't even come home for lunch. 'You go along,' he said, 'I'll eat later.'"

"He insisted. But don't say anything to him. He's trying to increase our profits. People do such things at first."

My husband and I laughed over the whole thing.

My *shoshur* appeared after my husband went back. Very excited, perspiring, his eyes glittering. No sooner had he set foot at home than he said, "This work is not for you,

Bouma. I sold seven saris today. All of them at high prices. One of them had fifty rupees written in a corner. Do you know what I did? I added a one. It was sold at one fifty. You see? Extra profits of a hundred rupees."

I sensed danger. The shop was just beginning to acquire a reputation. If the customer checked, he would come back either to argue or to return the sari. And he wouldn't shop here in the future. But how was I to explain this to my father-in-law? He was as joyful as a child with a new toy. He began to regale my *shaashuri* with stories about the shop, forgetting all about a bath and lunch.

Summoning me, my mother-in-law said, "Your shop will collapse now."

I smiled.

She said, "If you have any sense, you'll discourage him."

I said, "Never mind, we'll manage."

The next day he quarreled bitterly over the price with a couple of customers. They were regular buyers. "How can a sari that cost seventy-three rupees days ago cost a hundred and seventy now?" they complained. "This is daylight robbery." Whereupon my *shoshur* rolled up his sleeves to assault them. My husband had to intervene.

In the afternoon my father-in-law began his bluster,

"This is why I say shopkeeping is for the lower classes. People who aren't even worthy of carrying our shoes dare to argue with us."

My *shaashuri* said, "Why do you have to go to the shop then? Since you haven't done a day's work all your life, keep it that way. The household is running, isn't it?"

Flaring up in a rage, he said, "You think I can't do it?"

"Will you visit a shop where you're insulted?"

"A shopkeeper? Insult me? How dare he?"

"So you see, no customer will stomach a shopkeeper's insult. He has ten other shops he can visit."

"I have ten other customers to sell to."

"No, you don't. When one customer leaves because he's cheated, ten others follow him. Do you think shop-keeping is nothing but buying cheap and selling at a high price? If only it were that simple."

My *shoshur* glowered. He did continue going to the shop, but he didn't create any more trouble. Instead, he concentrated on learning the business despite his advanced age.

One day he said, "Look, Bouma, people love to bargain. They think they've won a huge victory if they can lower the price by two rupees. Your fixed-price shop doesn't give that opportunity. I suggest you do away with this fixed price. Raise the price a little, let the customer haggle for a price that will make them happy."

I said softly, "That's true."

He said happily, "Then shall we start tomorrow?"

"Why not? But the trouble is, most people know prices are fixed here. So no one will bargain other than new customers."

"That's true," he said, worried. "This will create problems."

He abandoned the idea on his own. I breathed a sigh of relief. Now he began to go to the shop both mornings and afternoons. To be honest, he ran the business quite smoothly. Every so often, he told me, "There's a thrill to it. The day passes so well, I meet new people, see new faces. It really is a new experience."

My *jaa* never came downstairs. She was bedridden with arthritis and high blood pressure. Even a whole year after the incident, she had not overcome her fear of me. So I never went upstairs either. My *bhaashur* would take her food to the first floor.

She sent for me one evening.

I went. Averting my gaze, she looked at the wall. Then she said, "Don't be angry. I want to say something. I have no choice but to say it."

I hadn't entered. I was standing at the doorstep, lest she was terrified. "Yes?" I said.

"We are in a bad way. My husband has no money. There's no gold to sell either. We can't go on."

"What do you suggest I do?"

"What can I tell you? You've rendered me useless with your black magic. You spared my life only out of kindness. But I am no longer afraid to die. Being tied to my bed is no different from being dead."

"I don't know any black magic."

Wiping her eyes with the end of her sari, she said, "It was only your kindness that you didn't make us starve. You know all sorts of spells and hypnotism; there's nothing you cannot do. I've been informed you've got your *shoshur* to work in your shop."

"You've been misinformed."

"I don't want to argue. You can do much more if you choose to. You can tear the family apart. I accept all this. But I cannot afford to be fearful. So I am speaking up."

"Explain in detail, Didi."

"I'm afraid to. But still I'm asking, have you sold all the jewelry?"

"Why do you ask?"

"I heard you've set up a huge shop. That needs lots of money."

"The money came from selling my own jewelry. I don't know about anyone else's."

"I'm not asking for a share. Don't be angry. I'm begging. If there's anything left over, please give me a little."

I knew greed was more powerful than fear. Greed teaches us how to overcome fear but not how to conquer it. My sister-in-law was terrified of me, but she couldn't control her greed.

She kept wiping her eyes. She said, "God will judge you for what you have done. But don't forget our claim. My husband is extremely embarrassed. He cannot bring himself to ask you. He's deep in penury. Even my treatment is about to be stopped."

"He's not all that old. He can easily work for a living if he wants to."

"Work for a living? How?"

"First he must feel the need to work."

She threw me a glance. Probably out of desperation. I saw hatred, revulsion, and fear in that fleeting look.

Averting her face again, she said, "He isn't highly educated. Who will give a job to someone who hasn't gone beyond high school? We don't have a jewelry box to start a shop with. You're talking of need? He has no opportunity even if he feels the need. All he says is that Fuchu has established himself, look how much money they're making, all we can do is watch. That's why I'm begging."

"What is it he wants to do?"

"Something. Anything. I don't know what." After a short silence, she lowered her voice. "You poisoned Pishima, took the jewelry box, but I haven't told anyone. I've stored the information like a scorpion stores poison. You should be grateful to me."

"Who told you I poisoned her?"

Seemingly afraid that I had asked this, she said, "Don't be angry. I'm not going to the police. I haven't even told your *bhaashur*. Isn't my silence worth anything to you?"

I didn't know what to say. Most people are in the habit of saying unnecessary things even when there is nothing to be said. I don't have that habit. I never speak when there is no need to. This time too I didn't try to defend myself or allay her suspicion. I knew she wouldn't believe me no matter what I said.

Without looking in my direction she said, "Have you left?"

"No. Are you done with me?"

"You haven't said anything. What should I assume?"

I stood in silence.

She looked at me again. Her eyes were blazing. She said, "That means you'll give us nothing? Nothing at all?"

I looked on in silence. An angry spark appeared in her eyes. She was aggressive by nature and had merely bottled up her hostility all this time. Now the lid had been lifted by the steam building up beneath it all this while.

Grinding her teeth, she said, "You witch. You want to gobble it all up. You think you can keep it all for yourself? I've lived in fear, indulged you all this while. No longer . . ."

Lifting her inert, diseased body off the bed simply with the fuel of her rage, she charged at me like a specter, her hair flying, her sari slipping off her shoulder.

To my astonishment, I found myself looking at greed, covetousness, envy, and loathing in human form. I couldn't move. She pounced on me like a tigress. "I'll kill you today . . . kill you . . . if I have to die afterward I will . . . I'll kill you first . . ."

"You grab her throat too," someone whispered in my ear.

My *jaa* seemed to be possessed by a demonic power. She began to throttle me with a pincer grip.

Pishima kept saying in my ear, "Do you want to die? Die then. Die, both of you. Why don't you grab her throat too? Lift your arms, Maagi. Ha, look at her standing like a cripple."

Trying with all my force to breathe and to pry my sister-in-law's hands off my throat, I said, "No, Pishima."

My *jaa* heard me say "No, Pishima." Her grip loosened. Staring at me with bulging eyes, she said, panting, "You witch! You're summoning spirits. Summoning ghosts. You can do anything. Anything. I'll kill you before I die, I'll kill you first. . . ."

Pishima whispered in my ear, "What are you standing there for? She will finish you. Grab her throat. Throttle her."

Tears were streaming down my face. I just stood there, making no effort to do anything.

Pishima went on: "You won't get this chance again. There's no one nearby. Throttle the *maagi*. Kill her. No one will know."

My sister-in-law continued her bluster, but she couldn't go on. She came toward me to grab my throat again, but her hands shook uncontrollably.

Pishima said, "Don't you understand, she will be a threat to you if she lives. She will kill you in your sleep one night. Finish the enemy now."

My *jaa* couldn't come up to me, falling on her face on the floor, all the strength in her sickly body exhausted. She sobbed loudly.

I went downstairs slowly.

At night I told my husband, "I want to start another shop."

He looked at me in surprise. "Another shop! I can barely manage this one. Ten to fifteen thousand in sales every day, I hardly even have time to sleep. Who's going to look after another shop?"

"We don't have a good shop hereabouts for radios and tape recorders," I pleaded. "I've heard Jagu Saha is selling his shop. Please find out."

My husband was staring at me. Suddenly he said, "What's that mark on your throat? Those angry red patches? You've cut yourself."

With a bowed head I told him, "If you care for me at all, do not ask more questions. Men don't have to know everything."

He looked grim. Then he said, "You want to conceal something? Very well."

It took me some time to restrain my tears. Then I said, "There's something I want to say."

"What is it?"

"We can be entirely happy only when we don't hear anyone else sighing sadly into our ears."

"That sounds philosophical," said my husband in surprise.

"But still true. Don't you agree?"

"Tell me what you want. I never turn you down, do I?"

"You are the best among men to me."

"You're going to ruin me one day with all these words," he said, smiling gently. "I might even start believing it of myself."

"You'll never understand where I get my strength from, how the forces of good take my hand even amid evil."

"Does the bruise on your throat tell such a story? Of good amid evil?"

I wept a little more. "I cannot be happy while others are not," I told him. "Why don't you ever think of your elder brother? He's in trouble."

"Dada! Why should Dada be in trouble? His household is running smoothly."

"What are you saying? What about male pride? Why should he be beholden to you? Give him a chance to earn for himself."

"So the new shop is for Dada? But can he run it?"

"You ran yours, didn't you?"

Embarrassing me thoroughly, he said, "That was thanks to you. I have you, Dada doesn't."

"He has you. Don't let anyone else in the family ever have to sigh again."

He examined my throat carefully. Then he said, "You've learned the art of keeping things from me these days."

Tearfully, I said, "No, I won't conceal anything. But everything has its time and place. Else even well-meant things cause harm. Information must be given at the appointed hour, on the appointed day. Not now. I'll tell you when the time is right."

Sighing, he said, "Very well. I will wait."

When the preparations for buying the shop began, my *shaashuri* sent for me and said, "I believe you're setting up a shop for your *bhaashur*."

I smiled but said nothing.

Putting her hand on my head, she said, "You have a kind heart. But there's something I have to tell you."

"What is it?"

"Your *bhaashur* is as vain as all the other men in this family. He might take your help because he is in trouble, but

95

it will pinch him all his life. And besides, it's your hard-earned money. You'll lose everything if the business fails."

"Everything will be all right, Ma."

"That's what you keep saying. I know the ways of this family very well. I still have some jewelry and gold coins I had kept hidden from everyone. My last resources. But they're of no use to me now. I have protected them from the wastrels of the family all this time. Sell these to pay for the shop. Your *bhaashur* will have no misgivings if you do this."

"But why, Ma? They're your last resources. Let them be."

"There's no point hoarding them either. Let them come to some use instead; let them spread some light. So long as they're not misused. You can give the shop to him, but you must keep an eye on it. I'm giving up my jewelry only because you're there."

I didn't object anymore.

Even my *bhaashur* seemed relieved when he was told. I saw a generous smile on his face.

He began running the shop. Every day I offered him some advice, very quietly and deferentially. He followed my suggestions without demurring. He was enjoying his time at the shop too. There was always music on the gramophone or the tape recorder or the radio, ensuring that there was no boredom.

Slowly, the shop began running.

One night someone woke me up from deep sleep. "Thief! Thief! Thieves breaking in! Wake up, wake up quickly. They'll take all I have, you wretch. I don't care what you lose, but if they take mine I'll bury you alive. . . ."

I shot up in bed. There were indeed two shadowy figures at the window near my head. They were sawing through the bars. As soon as I switched the torch on they vanished. I woke my husband up. There was an uproar, but the thieves weren't caught.

My husband went back to sleep, but I couldn't. I could see a hint of Pishima's white sari in the darkness.

"Why do you sleep like a bear, Maagi? Can't you guard the jewelry? Lying in your husband's arms! Die, die, die . . . Don't you have any shame? Always having fun! You dress like a whore in the evenings to seduce your husband. Why can't you get dropsy, why can't you get arthritis, why can't you get TB? You've turned a man from this family into a sheep . . . *thoo thoo thoo* . . . I spit on such love . . . *thoo thoo thoo* . . ."

Pishima prowled the room all night, constantly going

"*thoo thoo thoo.*" She was agitated, furious. Thieves had almost made off with her prized possessions.

I felt guilty. We lived on the ground floor of an old house, with over a hundred *bhoris* of gold in the room. A new servant and cook had been appointed. I ought to have been more careful.

I had a safe brought in the very next day. Pishima's jewelry went into it. The keys were in my safekeeping. We were making money. Sales at the shop exceeded twenty thousand on some days. The safe offered security from that point of view too.

Four years after getting married, I was finally touched by a trace of sin. It shook me to my foundations. A storm blew in to ravage my room with its open doors and windows.

My husband had to go to Calcutta frequently, Delhi and Bombay too, even Benaras and Kanchipuram. Our shop had grown. There were five employees. I didn't like procuring vast amounts of anything. I would tell my husband that products must be bought from the source, else we would appear old-fashioned and dull to customers. It would be more expensive too. Wholesalers were cheats.

My husband was no longer slothful like earlier. He was perpetually alert and active. Our products came from different parts of India. We dealt directly with weavers and mills. So my husband had to travel a lot these days. Long distances. During those periods, my father-in-law took over the shop in the morning and I in the afternoon.

On that occasion my husband was in South India. I was alone on a stormy night when I heard a melting voice.

"Can you hear me?"

"I can."

"A young man follows you every day. Have you noticed?"

"No!" I said, startled. "When does he follow me?"

"Don't pretend. Who's that man who follows you when you return from the shop every night? You think I don't know?"

"I haven't noticed anyone."

"Such a lovely boy. Eat him up. Gobble him up. To your heart's content. There's no such thing as sin in this world. Chastity is nonsense. Get rid of the idea. Eat him up."

My heart was thumping, my throat was dry.

"You're so pretty, why do you dress like a ragpicker? You don't comb your hair, you don't wear nice clothes, you're like a bad omen come home. Why, you stupid girl, are there no men in the world besides your husband?"

"Be quiet, Pishima. Even listening to all this is sinful."

"Aha, such a paragon of virtue. Sati and Savitri rolled into one. Why don't you dress up? A little lipstick, some kohl on your eyes, do up your hair, wear a bright sari—then you'll see. There'll be waves when you walk down the street."

"For shame, Pishima."

"Forget the shame. He stares at you so hungrily. Why do you want to deprive him, you husband eater? Do you think there's any such thing as sin? It's depriving your body that's a sin."

"Don't tell me any more. I don't want to hear."

Pishima filled the room with her icy chortling. My heart froze in fear.

The streets were desolate when I made my way back from the shop the next day. People in small towns did not venture out at this hour. I was looking straight ahead, but my mind was on what was behind me. Was there someone there? Was I really being followed?

Suddenly I looked behind me. That was when I saw him. A tall young man, dressed in pajamas and a panjabi. A head of unkempt hair, a light beard. His face was clearly visible in the bright pool of light from a shop. My husband was handsome, of course, but not so enchanting. A feudal nobility was evident in my husband's appearance, but this man was like a poem. Oval, doe-like eyes. Such a sweet pair of lips. He was walking slowly, his eyes on me.

I practically ran the rest of the way home, my heart hammering.

"Did you see him?" Pishima asked in the dead of night.

"*Chhih*, Pishima."

"Listen to me, the man at home is easy pickings. Like regular clothing. Piss in it, shit in it, wash and wear. But these men are like saris of fine silk. You must try them sometimes."

"For shame!"

"You're so beautiful, and yet you want to be on only one man's plate every time? What kind of woman are you? Even the gods and goddesses were up to so much more. Read the *Mahabharata*, you'll find out for yourself. Desire is like a river; it can sweep everything away. Just a matter of not getting caught. It will never lodge a complaint."

Tears sprang to my eyes.

I got one of the employees at the shop to accompany me home the next day. I didn't look backward even once. The next three days passed this way. On the fourth day I was alone again on my way home. It seemed silly to have a bodyguard. He wasn't going to attack me, after all. Let him follow me if he wanted to.

Barely had I taken a few steps than I knew that someone was behind me. Was it him?

I looked backward at an opportune moment. It was him. Today too his face was in the light. Why did my heart begin to thump?

No, I didn't run tonight. I walked home at a normal pace, with a trembling heart.

Late at night, Pishima's throbbing voice said, "Isn't he beautiful? Didn't I tell you? What's all this shyness for? There's no hurry. You have to entice him. Roll your hips. Smile saucily. Let your eyes speak. You haven't learned any tricks, you fool. Do you really like this dull man of yours? He's like a boiled egg. What has god given you so much for? You're pretty, you're accomplished, you have such flirtatious eyes. Go on, get your toes wet and see what it's like."

"Are you never going to let me alone, Pishima? What have I done to you?"

"Don't give me all this pious talk, you whore. I've seen many like you."

On the seventh day I couldn't contain myself any longer. I was on my way back from the shop. When I became aware that he was following me, my head pounded with fury. I wheeled around. Taken aback, he had to stop too. Marching up to him, I stood face-to-face and shouted at him. "What do you want? Why do you follow me every day?"

He was so flustered that he could only stare at me in bewilderment. Then, saying something unintelligible, he lowered his head and practically ran away.

I was just twenty-two. In full bloom. But my anxieties about the family and all my responsibilities had made me forget how young I was. I felt like the oldest of old women. I didn't care about my appearance or about dressing up. My entire being seemed to be centered around one individual. But today my age seemed to call out to me; my forgotten youth seemed to send me reminders. I felt beautiful, and I heard my beauty asking me, "Should we go back empty-handed?"

Returning in the dead of night, Pishima asked, "So you talked to him?"

"No. I scolded him."

Going off into peals of laughter, Pishima said, "Well done! It's good to be distant at first. It'll make him hungrier. Men are such gluttons. Make him thrash about in the water before you reel him in. Then shut the door and eat him up. Turn him into pulp."

I covered my ears with my hands.

"I've seen plenty of chaste women. All starving in silence. Put on the green silk sari tomorrow. You look pretty in it. Don't use so much red *sindoor* in your hair part. Look a little unmarried."

"Go away, Pishima."

"Why should I? Do I live on your father's charity? Radha was no less pious than you. Does that mean she didn't do anything with Krishna? Would she have done it if it was a sin?"

My heart was on fire. I stared into space all night. What did he want? Why did he follow me?

He shadowed me the next day too. But from a distance. I spotted him. I wanted to weep. Why was he going to so much trouble? Why did he show up every day despite this humiliation? What did he have to gain?

Two days later it rained. The first showers at the end of summer. The roads became wet. The air cooled.

The clouds dissipated to reveal an exquisite moon in the sky. Not an everyday moon. It seemed to have floated in from a fairy-tale realm. A thousand fragments appeared on the leaves, on the glistening streets, in small puddles.

As soon as I stepped out, I realized it was a drunken

night. Loveliness would not be thwarted tonight. It was a night of extremes. Of wild winds. No one was willing to behave themselves. Everything had been turned upside down. An alchemist had recast the ingredients of the world to create a completely new universe. The sky had never held so many stars, had it? Perhaps I had been borne away somewhere on the breeze, on a moonbeam.

Turning around tenderly, I saw no one behind me. He was not following me. Had he chosen this maddening moonlit night not to come? Tonight I seemed to have been expecting him too. I felt a little saddened, a little sour. I'd become used to him, after all.

Muttering my disapproval at the empty street, I walked slowly. There was no hurry to get anywhere. Maybe he would come. Maybe it wasn't too late.

He wasn't behind me. He was in front. Startling me, he suddenly blocked my way on that desolate road. His tall frame, doe-like eyes, a giant moon above his head. I had stopped in enchanted wonder, unknown to myself. Gazing at him shamelessly. Such deep ardor in his look! What infinite passion in that pair of lips!

His eyes were boring into me. Waves of silence passed back and forth between the two of us for some time.

Suddenly he spoke, the words falling off his lips. "I . . . I love you."

He couldn't remain after this. Filled with dread, he disappeared after setting off an explosion. I had nothing to say in response anyway. But the walls were being razed within me. The mountains were crumbling. The way was no longer clear.

I went home on slow footsteps, as though I had no destination, nowhere to arrive, ever. It even took me some effort to identify my own front door. Was this where I lived? Was this my address?

I flooded my pillow that night with my tears.

Pishima said intensely, "Cry. It will wash the grime away. Duties and rituals and caste and religion are all grime. Let it all be swept away. Then you can cross the river. You will see the joy it brings."

"Joy, Pishima! I'm burning within."

"Let it all be burned to ashes, all the garbage."

I stared into the darkness all night, my eyes flaming.

When I opened the front door early the next morning, I found that someone had left a rain-soaked, bloodred rose by the doorstep, complete with its stem and green leaves. It hadn't bloomed yet.

I picked the rose up, putting it in my room. Let it blossom. Let the flower bloom.

He chased me every day. Every morning he left a bloodred rose on my doorstep. Was this a sin? Was this what it meant to be cut from my moorings and have my boat adrift on a mad current?

My exhausted husband came back at dawn one day. Opening the door, I said in utter surprise when I saw him, "It's you at last? Where were you all these days? Why do you leave me alone?"

Bursting into tears, I knocked my head over and over against his chest.

Putting his arms around me, he said, "What's all this? Don't cry. You know I went for work."

"Don't leave me and go away ever again."

The bloodred rose lay on the doorstep that day too. Not having seen it, my husband ground it beneath his heel as he entered.

I didn't pick the rose up.

That night I put fresh sheets on the bed, arranged the pillows, and scattered flower petals. A little perfume too.

When he came to bed, he said, "This looks like it's our wedding night."

I embraced him hungrily. Inarticulately, I said, "Give me."

"What's all this, Lata? You know everything I have is yours."

"I want you more. More. Give me you."

A restless voice floated around the room. "So you didn't cross the line? You didn't go for your tryst? Die of cholera, die of typhoid. I'll turn into a snake and bite your husband. You'll die, you'll die."

I drew my husband into bed. I couldn't delay any longer. My eyes were flowing with tears. My heart was burning away.

The voice kept cursing me: "Eat him up, eat him up, eat him up, eat him up. . . ."

Closing my eyes, I held my husband tightly, my lips on his. In my head I said, "Be quiet, temptation, be still, my beating heart. Be born. Be born through us. Let your pain recede, let your agony end. . . ."

The sound circled the bed. "Eat him up, eat him up, eat him up, eat him up. . . ."

I said, "Let the flames in your heart go out, let the torment of your desire be calmed, let the anguish of your self-repression be relieved. Serenity. This is your moment of birth. Be tranquil, this is a beautiful moment. Fill my arms, fill my heart. Be born, be born, be born. . . ."

The sound faded. Forever. Our union reached a climax.

Nine months later I gave birth to a daughter. She was born in spring, in *boshonto*. We called her Boshon.

There was no sign of Pishima anywhere in the house. No sound. Calmness. Unburdened.

I couldn't stop looking at Boshon. She lay on her bed like a bouquet of flowers. That's how beautiful she was. Hugging and kissing her, I asked sometimes, "Do you recognize me? Do you recognize this house? Don't you remember anything?"

The baby gazed at me uncomprehendingly.

A child had been born in the family after a very long time. A furious tug-of-war broke out over her. My *shaashuri* gave up on her gods and goddesses to spend all her time with her granddaughter. My *shoshur* skipped the shop frequently. Even his elder brother, who would seldom come downstairs, went into the living room often. My *bhaashur* was so charmed by his niece that he filled the room with toys. Boshon was passed around from one person's arms to another's, being cuddled all the time. Since no one was willing to set her down on the floor, she didn't learn how to crawl and walked rather late.

But all this while, my *jaa* didn't even set eyes on Boshon.

She was unable to climb down the stairs. Arthritis, high blood pressure, and all sorts of other illnesses surrounded her joylessly.

One afternoon, when Boshon had just learned to toddle around, she slipped past everyone's eyes and climbed upstairs. She stood at my *jaa*'s door on tottering legs, observing her with great surprise while she sucked her thumb.

When my *jaa* spotted Boshon, she shouted, "Who's there? Who is it?"

It took her some time to realize that this was the daughter of the witch. She waved the baby away from her bed. "Go away! Go away from here."

Children understand clearly where they are not wanted. Scared, Boshon tried to turn and go back. But she tripped and rolled all the way to the bottom of the stairs.

Who knew how my *jaa*'s body was electrified, but she practically flew out of her bed and ran down the stairs to pick Boshon up. Boshon was blue with pain.

By the time Panchu, the family servant, went upstairs, alarmed by the sounds, my *jaa* was cradling Boshon in her arms and crying as she applied a cold compress to the injured area.

I wasn't home. I heard about it from my *shaashuri* when

I returned later in the afternoon. Looking woebegone and guilty, she said, "Such a turbulent girl. I'd gone for my bath when she went upstairs. And then . . ."

"Is she in Didi's room?" I asked with fear and trepidation.

"Yes, she's still there. Who knows what's going on? Your *jaa*'s heart is full of poison. Send Panchu to fetch your daughter."

After a short silence, I said, "Let it be, Ma."

The cook appeared and said, "The *boudi* has asked for some rice to feed Boshon. Shall I take her some rice?"

"Yes," I told him.

After this Boshon began to visit her *boudi* upstairs every day. There was no one in the family she didn't win over.

When she was alone with me I still looked for signs on her face. "Don't you remember the jewelry box?" I asked her. "Don't you remember the pain, the suffering? Don't you remember any of it?"

I had no idea what Boshon babbled in reply.

 PART FOUR

BOSHON

cannot explain how barren the second floor feels. I occupy three enormous rooms. My mother doesn't like that I live here by myself. An entire terrace and as many as three coveted rooms had lain vacant for a long time. They would be swept and cleaned and then put back under lock and key. I demanded that I be allowed to move in.

They tried to dissuade me, even scolded me. But eventually I did get my three-room kingdom on the second floor. Ma and Baroma used to spend the nights with me at first, in case I felt frightened. But I feel no fear at all. I love living alone. I can sense an eerie desolation blowing through the three rooms and the terrace all day long. It's not the wind, but who knows what it is that whistles through the rooms.

The entire floor is packed with furniture. A huge, heavy bedstead, several large wooden wardrobes, a marble-top table, a big clock with a pendulum on the wall. Dolls lined up in a glass case. All of these had belonged to a great-aunt of mine who died before I was born. What a tragic life she had! Married at seven, widowed at twelve. How fortunate I wasn't born in that time! My god, what a horrible system. No wonder women are rebelling for freedom.

My friends visit me sometimes. They're astonished to see what a big space I live in. Some of them envy me too. And a few say, "Oh, lord, I'd die of fear if I had to live here alone. How do you manage? So brave, honestly."

There was a big discussion one evening. Suddenly Chanchal said, "Look, Boshon, you could be kidnapped."

I said in surprise, "Kidnap? Who'll kidnap me?"

"It suddenly occurred to me last night, my god, Boshon is the perfect target. They have so much money, and she's the apple of everyone's eye. Considering the times we live in, criminals can easily kidnap Boshon."

Indrani said, "No one will kidnap her. But the danger for Boshon lies elsewhere."

"Where?"

"Anyone who marries her will get a kingdom of sorts, right? I bet lots of people will want to marry her."

She wasn't wrong. My *jethu,* my father's brother, has no children. I am the only child of my parents. Everything will come to me.

Tilak said, "It's not for nothing Mr. Chatterjee, a respected lawyer, wanted to marry her. It's true, Boshon, you have to be very careful."

He spoke with so much authority that we started laughing. I said, "Want a slap? You think they all want to marry me only for my money and nothing else?"

"You have an excess of everything, honestly," said Jhinuk. "There's divine justice for you."

Bachhu said dispassionately, "Boshon is beautiful all right, but that classical beauty doesn't work in this day and age."

I asked in surprise, "Are you saying I'm worthless?"

"I'm not saying that," Bachhu replied knowledgeably, "but those aristocratic almond-shaped eyes and plump cheeks and lustrous curls are not valued anymore. Tastes have changed. Haven't you seen—it's girls with prominent jaw lines and sunken eyes and sharp cheekbones who are chosen as heroines for the movies these days."

Irked, Tilak said, "Forget it. It's beneath our dignity to discuss people's appearances. Beauty is skin-deep. Personality is the main thing."

In my head I withdrew from the chatter to think about myself. Why did I have an excess of everything? Money, looks, doting family, friends. It tires me out sometimes. My entire family keeps its eyes on me. I used to have two *dadus*, my father's father and his uncle. Both of them had spoiled me. They died within a year of each other, but that hasn't made the others dote any less on me.

Ma is the only one I can set apart from the rest. She loves me to no end, but she doesn't indulge me. My mother is a strange person, actually. We hardly have anything in common.

Even my friends say, "Your mother's very odd, isn't she? See how much she still cares for her husband?"

It's true that none of my friends has parents so devoted to each other. Ma is full of reverence and respect for Baba, deferring to him in a way I'm incapable of. And yet it is this old-fashioned woman who runs the entire household flawlessly. I've heard that it was her effort and enterprise that led to these two shops we own. Our affluence today is the result of her farsightedness. Everyone swears by her.

She is the one who rescued the family from collapse and set it back on its feet.

The formal way in which Ma addresses Baba does not seem unusual to me for I've been hearing it from my childhood. But it grates on my friends' ears. They ask me, "Why does your mother address your father formally, as Aapni?"

I felt embarrassed then. I asked my mother, "Why do you address Baba as Aapni, Ma?"

She told me, "He was so much older than me, such personality. Aapni seemed natural. Not that it did any harm."

"Should everyone address their husbands that way?"

"Of course not. To each according to their own. But my strength comes from the fact that I have always respected him. Otherwise everything would have fallen apart."

I didn't understand this. But I didn't ask Ma any more questions either. This house is still imprisoned in an old, feudal atmosphere. The world outside is changing so fast.

When I woke up this morning on the second floor, the winter sun was flooding the room through the eastern window. The day was well advanced. But my head was still full of last night's moonlight and desolation.

As I was about to go downstairs after brushing my teeth, I discovered Baroma climbing up the stairs. Her rheumatic knee makes it difficult for her. She was panting.

I said, "Why must you come upstairs, Baroma? All you have to do is call."

"What were you telling the Chatterjee woman so loudly last night,?"

I chuckled. "I'm glad I did. Why do they torture her?"

"Why do you have to interfere in other people's affairs? Do you want to start a fight with them? You were shouting! The entire neighborhood must have heard. You mustn't do such things."

"I really want to get all my friends together and attack their house one day."

"You're quite capable of it. There's nothing you can't do. They said you even pushed a lorry last night."

"We'd have had to spend the night on the road if we didn't push the lorry."

Baroma's eyes turned to saucers. "What next? I've never heard of girls pushing lorries."

"Do you think we're still living in your era, Baroma? Girls today can do everything."

"Do anything, do everything, just don't stop being a girl. Don't turn into a boy. The way things are going, I'll be grateful if women don't start sprouting beards."

I couldn't contain my laughter. "The things you say, Baroma! You're jealous of today's girls, aren't you?"

"That's true, I am a bit." Baroma fished out a small bowl from somewhere beneath the end of her sari. "Eat these. I just made them."

Gokul pithe. Those palm-sugar-and-coconut savories I abominate. My nose began to wrinkle inadvertently. But telling her that was out of the question. All I could say was, "You won't give up till I'm a ball of pudding, will you?"

"*Oma!* Listen to the girl. Why should you be a ball?"

"Of course I will. Do you know how many calories these sweets have?"

"Never heard of such a thing. Eat. You have to eat these in winter. It's a special day."

"You know what I love?"

"Only too well. Those things that wriggle like worms and spicy *shingaras* from Gopal's shop. No wonder you're turning into a skeleton."

"Skeletons are in demand these days. I'm going to open

my mouth, and pop it in. No way I'm touching that syrupy stuff. My hand will get icky."

"Open wide. It's hot. Be careful."

Truth to tell, I'm closer to Baroma than to Ma. Baroma is an open book; she can't keep anything to herself. Her affection for me includes force-feeding, antislimness propaganda, even opposition to feminism. Still, I can win her over whenever I want. I can ask for anything and get it too.

Baroma almost fainted when Jethu bought me a scooter a year and a half ago. She had a huge fight with him. Apparently she had never seen such a thing in her life. Now she rides on the seat behind me.

Baroma says, "You're actually a boy. You were born a girl by mistake."

Baroma has no idea how much of a girl I am. I don't have the slightest regret about being a girl, though she may. I'm very happy to have been born a girl. If there's such a thing as rebirth, I want to be born a girl every time. I want the world to belong only to women. There's no need for men. What a lovely world it would have been with women alone! But then, no, not without Baba and Jethu and my two *dadus*. They will be the only four males on earth. Baba, Jethu, and my two *dadus*. No one else.

It was a holiday. I had lots of things to do. Music lessons, go to Shabari's for science notebooks and then to Sumita's—she was knitting a cardigan for me, and I had to ask her to change the design a bit.

As soon as I went downstairs, Ma said, "Boshon, come to my room after breakfast."

Was she sounding grim? My mother is a little grim.

Ma's room is dark and dingy, horrible. And packed with trunks and cases and who knows what else. Baroma was perched on the bed, her legs dangling. Ma was in front of the safe. A huge jewelry box lay on the floor in front of her.

"Shut the door and come here."

I shut the door and remained standing.

Ma gave me a peculiar look. "Do you recognize this box? Remember anything?"

I shook my head. "No. What should I remember?"

"This box was yours once."

I looked away in disgust. "I have no idea."

"Maybe not in this lifetime."

I looked at Ma in astonishment. My mother was always

rational. I've never heard her spout mumbo jumbo. What did this mean?!

"You mean in another lifetime?"

Baroma told Ma in irritation, "Why do you have to spell everything out? You're a fool."

Ma opened the lid. "Take a look. Check everything."

The box was filled with old, heavy jewelry. Made me want to throw up. Ugly things.

"There's nothing to check," I said. "Ancient ornaments."

"More than a hundred *bhoris*. Nothing less."

"Why are you showing me all this? I have enough jewelry. Have you seen me wear any of it? I hate ornaments."

"It was my responsibility. That's why."

"Whom does all this belong to? Did you get it when you got married?"

"No. It's all yours."

"I don't want it. Keep it."

Ma's face brightened for a moment even in that dark room. She seemed to emit a suppressed but anxious sigh.

Baroma said, "Can you stop all this drama of yours, Lata? Heaven knows what madness takes hold of you sometimes. She's a little girl—what do they know of jewelry these days? Call Kshitish and ask him to remake some of these. Not too many. Best not to show jewelers how much gold you have at home."

I could make no sense of this morning performance. I looked at them by turn. What did all this mean?

Why was Ma staring at me? I wasn't new around here.

Ma said, "I took the box out with your permission."

"My permission? Why, Ma? I've never seen this jewelry in my life. Whose is it?"

Ma lowered her head. "Someone has bequeathed this to you. It was in my safekeeping all this time, that's all."

"What'll I do with it? Who bequeathed it to me?"

"A *thakuma*, a great-aunt, of yours. She had a sad life. This jewelry was like her heart."

"Who was she?"

"You haven't seen her. Rashomoyee."

I smiled. "I've seen her photos. So beautiful. It's her rooms I'm occupying, isn't that so?"

"You're there by right. Why should you be occupying them?"

"Why did you bring these out today?"

Ma and Baroma exchanged mysterious glances. I scented a mild conspiracy.

"I have to go, Ma. Lots to do."

SHIRSHENDU MUKHOPADHYAY

"All right."

No one can understand the romantic madness of putting on a helmet and floating away on a scooter. The sharp cold wind entering my brain through my nose and mouth swept away all thoughts of the jewelry. I simply cannot understand Ma and Baroma. So old-fashioned. Obsessed with nothing but gold and ornaments. Do they ever try to find out how beautiful the world is?

It was afternoon by the time I got to Sumita's after visiting a couple of other places. Parking the scooter, I entered, saying, "Sumita, *ei* Sumita."

A tall, gentle young man was sitting on a sofa in the drawing room. Tender beard. Unkempt hair. Faraway expression. He had changed a lot, but I wouldn't forget him in my entire life. I came to an abrupt halt. My heart stopped beating for a few moments. And then the memories of humiliation came marauding from the past like soldiers on a rampage.

A deep, resonant voice said, "Sumita? She's probably upstairs."

I left the room and went up the stairs without any awareness of what I was doing.

A disheveled Sumita was sprawled on her bed amid a

126

sea of wool. As soon as she saw me, she said in a forlorn voice, "Haven't finished today either. What to do? Dada came back after such a long time. We're having so much fun. No time for anything else. Come, sit here. Did Dada see you?"

I nodded.

"Did you talk to him?"

"Why?"

Sumita concentrated on her knitting needles. "Just asking."

She wasn't just asking. I could see a faint pattern in all this. I was hardening, getting angry. But I couldn't say anything.

Sumita said softly, "He's been in America so long. Imagine what a hard time he's had. It was very tough at first."

I had no use for all this information. So I did not respond.

Sumita said, "I heard your lorry broke down on the road last night."

"Yes."

"What a shame I couldn't go this year. Dada's home. How could I go? So much to talk about."

"So you talk to your brother these days? You used to be afraid of him."

"Dada wasn't the way he is now. Nor are we. We've grown up."

"Is your brother less conceited now?"

Sumita's face fell.

After a short silence, she said, "Conceited. What did Dada ever have to be conceited about? We barely had enough to eat. Had to borrow things all the time. Dada was so shy he could never ask. We never knew when he was hungry. The truth is, he has suffered a lot."

"Good."

"Is that what you think of him?"

"I know nothing about Amalesh-da. What should I think about him?"

"You said he was conceited."

"He was a good student; he could easily have been conceited."

"Don't say that. He used to send most of his scholarship money from America to us. He starved himself. Studied all the time."

"Why do I need to know all this?"

"No one has ever said anything bad about Dada."

"Bring the cardigan home when it's done. But don't make it long sleeved. Try three-quarters."

Sumita nodded. "All right. But I'll be a bit late. Because Dada's here."

Sumita came downstairs to see me off. As I was putting on my helmet, I heard her tell her brother discreetly, "This is Boshon, Dada."

The deep voice said, "I know."

Today the old humiliation was stinging me like nettle. I kept grinding my teeth. I had never driven my scooter so fast. My house was close by, just three doors away. But I had gathered so much speed that I couldn't stop in time. I had to brake hard. The scooter reared up like a horse. And then it went in one direction while I was flung in another. My left arm was badly hurt. Tears sprang to my eyes. But by the time I left my ignominious bed of dust, my heart was in more pain than my body.

Lifting the scooter from where it lay on the ground, I wheeled it home slowly before a crowd could gather.

Back in the privacy of the second floor, I found my left arm bruised all the way to the elbow. It was bleeding profusely. I had injured my head too, but not too badly thanks to the helmet. Was there an injury to the hip too?

Probably. But none of these could affect me physically. I went to my room and sat quietly in my chair. As though I was possessed. There was a wailing in my heart that went beyond the usual sounds of the second floor. A keen wailing that left me bereft.

I would be scolded roundly if found out and not allowed to ride my scooter anymore. So I had to clean the wound and put antiseptic cream on it. Luckily, it was winter, which let me put on a long-sleeved blouse. But not every wound can be kept out of sight. Why did that insolent silence in response to an innocent letter written in the foolishness of puberty have to come back multiplied a thousand times today?

There was a new restaurant in town. It had become quite famous. Jethu took me there in the evening. A swank, flashy place. A superb restaurant, really, considering it was a small town.

Jethu had just been diagnosed with high blood sugar. He was under restrictions. I glared at him. "You mustn't eat anything you want. Give me the menu, I'll pick for you."

Jethu pulled a long face. "One meal does no harm."

"No, Jethu, high blood sugar is dangerous. Stew and salad for you. With two tandoori rotis."

"Two spoons of fried rice?"

"All right, from my plate."

"What's the matter with you? You look pale."

"Why do all of you keep an eye on me all the time, Jethu? Don't you have anything better to do?"

"Never mind, eat now."

Jethu looked like he wanted to say something. He tried several times but couldn't.

It was a lovely evening. After a delicious meal, Jethu took me to play video games. I don't know what was wrong, but I couldn't score well at all.

At night, a symphony of pain took over my body, the agony jangling like a musical instrument. I hadn't realized the extent of the injury. Did I have a fever? I was feeling unusually cold. More than that, something was blowing across the room. What was it?

I couldn't sleep. Getting out of bed, I switched on the lights in all three rooms and then wandered between them like a wraith. My great-aunt, Rashomoyee the child widow, used to roam around these rooms once upon a time. There was nothing for her to savor in her life, no joy. She wasn't allowed to eat at a restaurant or ride a scooter or play video games. All she did was rummage through her jewelry. And sigh. And hold hands with loneliness. Was it the void in her heart that was flitting about the room tonight? Was it her sighs I could hear?

There was a huge mirror on the wardrobe door. I sat down in front of it on a stool. Dada used to say, "Boshon resembles Rashomoyee."

I do. I know I do. There are some photographs of Rashomoyee's in the family album. Taken late in her life. Still, the face doesn't change with age. A flawless beauty. I was feeling sad for Rashomoyee tonight. She had apparently bequeathed her jewelry to me. So strange. How did she know I would be born?

I couldn't get out of bed in the morning. My arm was aching, my hips were frozen with pain, my head was throbbing. The signs of a high fever were there in my body. And over and above all this, that same wailing even on this sunlit winter morning. The same sense of feeling bereft.

The entire family would pounce on me if they found out I was unwell. Doctors, medicines, permanent security in the form of Ma and Baroma in the room. A bigger pain. I didn't tell them about little illnesses.

I was getting ready to go to college. Baroma came in. "College?"

"Yes, Baroma."

"Good."

She wanted to say something. The burned child fears the fire. That expression, this redundant question of whether I was going to college—I knew the signs only too well.

"Have you heard, Jatin Bose's eldest son is back."

"That's hardly news to me, Baroma. Sumita is my friend."

"Yes, of course. Very nice boy."

My heart wailed again. I adjusted my sari instead of responding.

Baroma said, "They were saying they're looking for a match for him."

Turning to her, I smiled. "What is it you want to say, Baroma?"

Baroma looked flustered. "No, that's not what I was suggesting. It was your *jethu* who was saying, he's a good boy. Comes from a poor family, struggled so hard to get where he has."

"I could guess, Baroma."

"Are you upset?"

"No. Why should I be angry with you? But for heaven's sake, don't make a proposal in any circumstances."

"But why not?"

"There are reasons."

The fever rose when I was in college. Never mind paying attention in class, there was a constant lamentation in my ear. A void in my heart. I sat down beneath a tree with the sun on my back during a break. Priti sat beside me, babbling about her Nitish. On and on. I paid no attention. All I could hear was the wailing in my heart. What was so attractive about a home and a family anyway?

Suddenly I turned to Priti and asked her cruelly, "How much does this Nitish of yours love you?"

Priti said in embarrassment, "You have no idea. He's so crazy. Apparently he thinks of me with every breath."

"Tell me, Priti, suppose someone suddenly threw an acid bulb at you and your face was burned horribly and you lost an eye. Suppose you became grotesquely ugly. Would your Nitish still marry you? Would he still love you?"

Priti's expression was indescribable. She gaped at me

for a few moments. Then she shrieked, "*Maago*! Are you a witch? Who says such nasty things?"

Chewing on a blade of grass, I said absently, "Is there any value to conditional love, which depends on your beauty or your position? I don't believe in it, you know. I don't believe in such love at all. Lovers have very fragile relationships."

"You're a demon. My heart is in my mouth. Have you any idea what you just said?"

"Think about it, Priti."

"I feel miserable."

"You're a fool. So you'll be happy. You can't be happy in life unless you're a fool." At that Priti left.

Jethu suddenly cleared his throat as we were eating at the enormous dining table that night and said, "I have something to ask you, Boshon. Think carefully before answering."

I stopped eating. Looking at him, I said, "I know what you're going to say. My answer is no. Never."

Everyone exchanged glances and fell silent.

"All right," Jethu said very softly. "But the boy's been waiting a long time. Apparently he had no plans of getting married. But when his family started pressuring him, he said, 'There's someone I've been waiting for all this time.'" Jethu paused and sighed. "Never mind. It's best to let them know we don't want this."

I went to my room. Desolation wailed from every corner. What was wrong with me?

Sumita appeared one afternoon a couple of days later, on another holiday. Her face was drawn. She said, "Try it on, see if it fits."

I put the cardigan on in front of the wardrobe. It was lovely. Sumita knitted very well.

"Do you like it?"

"Very much."

Sumita sat down. She said, "I stayed up two nights to finish the cardigan. I told myself, It's very cold, Boshon will find it hard without the cardigan."

I curled my lips, feeling guilty. "Rubbish, there was no hurry. I have so many."

"You think I don't know that? Still I imagined you were waiting for this one. You wanted it, after all."

"Why did you take so much trouble?"

"It's a joy to take trouble for some people. Is there anything your family hasn't done for us? It was Somlata whom Ma would turn to every time we ran short of something."

"I get angry when I hear all this, Sumi. Those who have enough can easily give some away. What's so great about it?"

Sumita was silent for some time. Then she said, "There was something Somlata used to say that I really liked. She would say, 'I can't take it when other people sigh.'"

I know my mother is a generous woman, I know. I will probably never achieve her greatness. So much respect for her husband, her bonds with the household, the way she battled poverty—no, I will never be able to match her, to be so devoted, so good like her.

Suddenly Sumita said, "Dada is leaving tomorrow."

I posed in front of the mirror, examining the cardigan.

Sumita said softly, "You turned him down?"

I didn't answer.

"We had no idea it was you he likes," Sumita said with moist eyes. "Who knows why? I asked him many times, 'When did you even set eyes on Boshon, Dada? You never look at girls.' He wasn't even around. I asked him, 'When did you start liking Boshon?' Dada just says, 'You won't understand. She has a score to settle with me.'"

Sumita continued, "I don't know what he means. Do you?"

I didn't know. All I could hear was the deathly current of the wails. Why was it coming from my heart? It rose above all other sounds.

"So many marriage proposals! Dada's turned them all down." Sumita sighed.

Suddenly I understood. The wailing in my heart only got worse when he was mentioned. A wild idea occurred to me, and I lowered my voice, sounding grave.

"Listen, Sumi, can you tell your brother something in complete confidence?"

"Tell him what?"

"First you have to swear to me you won't tell anyone else."

"You're frightening me. All right, I swear. Nothing bad, right?"

"It's bad. You touched me just now. Go home and wash your hands with disinfectant."

Startled, Sumita asked, "But why?"

"Listen, I'm telling you because I trust you. I haven't told anyone at home. They'll make a huge fuss if I do. You know how they care for me."

"Tell me, Boshon. I'm terrified now."

I put on a wonderfully convincing act. Without warning, I hid my face in the end of my sari and burst into tears. Then, still sobbing, I said, "I have leprosy."

"Oh, my god."

"I've been to the doctor in secret. I haven't told anyone."

Sumita sat like a stone.

After weeping for some time, I unveiled my tear-soaked face and said hoarsely, "Tell your brother."

Sumita was staring at me in fright. Then she said, "How did it happen? Are you sure?"

I rolled up my left sleeve and showed her my arm. It was already looking nasty with all the cream smeared on the wound. On top of which Sumita didn't even dare look properly. She hid her face. Perhaps she had tears in her eyes too.

When that fool, Sumita, had left with a face like thunder, perhaps I should have laughed to myself. But I wanted to cry instead. Why could I not trust love?

When I was young, I would often see a blood-red rose that someone would leave outside our door early in the morning every day. When I grew older, I learned that it was someone who had fallen in love with my mother. Unrequited, of course. He would leave a symbol of his bleeding heart outside the door every day. I would open the door at dawn so that I could claim the rose. One day, I opened the door a little too early. I saw the man. Tall and nice looking, with a rose in his hand. He was taken aback when he saw me. Then he smiled in embarrassment. Thrusting the rose into my hand, he left without a word. How wonderful it had felt that day.

It's been a long time since anyone has left a rose on our doorstep. Why did he give up? Does love dwindle? Does it get tired? Does love feel afraid? Could I ever accept love?

That night after bidding Sumita farewell, I returned home. Our house falls unnaturally silent every evening. My second-floor room was even more silent. Only a stream of pain, of separation, flowed through it. The wailing in my heart hadn't stopped.

Suddenly a sound broke through the silence. I heard footsteps coming up the stairs. They were not familiar ones. I was alarmed. How could someone just come up-stairs uninvited?

I knew who was coming. I didn't know how I knew. Was this supposed to be the way into my heart? Why did he have to be here, barging in, demolishing my resistance, my fear, my rejection?

I jumped up from my desk and ran deep into my room. I stood silently in the dark. My eyes were flowing with tears.

The footsteps had stopped at my doorstep. The constant wailing in my heart had disappeared somewhere.

ABOUT THE AUTHOR

Shirshendu Mukhopadhyay was born in 1935 in present-day Bangladesh. He earned a master's degree from Calcutta University and worked for some time as a schoolteacher before becoming a journalist and author. *The Aunt Who Wouldn't Die* is a much-loved contemporary classic in Bengali, and it was adapted into the film *Goynar Baksho* in 2013. The first English translation was published in India in 2017.

A NOTE FROM THE TRANSLATOR

Probably the greatest challenge in translating *The Aunt Who Wouldn't Die* was to find a voice in English for the ghost of Pishima, the dead aunt. In the patriarchal tradition-bound joint family in which she spent her living years, anything like a feminist spirit would have been crushed ruthlessly. She had to die in order to acquire some agency and significantly influence events in the family. In death, she acquires a profane tongue and a delightful lack of hesitation in using it. And so, the translation had to capture her intent and spontaneity in deploying swear words and her distinctly vengeful hostility toward the rest of the family, while keeping her character constant after death.

At one level, using scatology to achieve all of this was a delicious enterprise. It's not every day that a translator can dip into the gutter running through their heads in search of suitable words while performing a literary enterprise. But it was also a matter of making cultural choices in a language that the character in question would probably never have used in her life. Adding to the piquancy of the problem was the fact that the Bengali sensibility does not allude to sex directly, working instead through metaphor and innuendo.

In many senses, this cultural gap pervades all translations from Bengali into English, the language of the colonial masters of earlier generations of Bengali-speaking people. English is still considered a language of power compared to Bengali and, in some way, transferring a Bengali text into English is to automatically place its entire structure in a different position in the power hierarchy. Of course, this is something that only affects the India reader, since most readers around the world are not aware of the historical relationship between these languages. Still, it is an intellectually nagging factor for the translator, and it is important not to allow this discomfort to color the actual translation.

—Arunava Sinha

Here ends Shirshendu Mukhopadhyay's
The Aunt Who Wouldn't Die.

The first edition of this book was printed and
bound at LSC Communications in
Harrisonburg, Virginia, July 2020.

A NOTE ON THE TYPE

The text of this novel was set in Perpetua, a serif typeface
designed by Eric Gill, an English sculptor and printmaker
associated with the Arts and Crafts movement. It was
commissioned by Stanley Morison, the highly influential
typography advisor of the British Monotype Corporation.
Unlike many other designs of that period, which were ad-
aptations of classical typefaces, Perpetua was intended as
a contemporary type based entirely upon the needs and
conventions of modern England. Several of its features
derive from Gill's experience of carving letters on stone
monuments. It was released to the printing trade in 1932
and has proved a design of enduring quality and utility.

HarperVia

An imprint dedicated to publishing international voices,
offering readers a chance to encounter other lives and other
points of view via the language of the imagination.